A Dark Claim

A REAPERS OATH SERIES

PEG N. GREMLIN

For the ones who crave chaos, kiss monsters, and never apologize for setting the world on fire just to feel warm—this story is yours.

To the broken girls who stitched themselves back together with rage, who smiled through cracked lips and sharpened their teeth on survival—I see you. I wrote this for the version of you that still wonders if love can find you where the light doesn't reach.

To the readers who know that love isn't always soft. Sometimes it comes wrapped in shadows, blood-stained promises, and hands that grip too tightly. Sometimes it's a monster's devotion that saves you, not a hero's mercy.

To the wicked, the wild, and the ones who never begged quietly—thank you for existing. You are my people.

You are my light in the dark. You remind me daily why I believe in stories, even the twisted ones. Keep dreaming, keep questioning, and never let the world dim your spark.

And to the version of me that wrote this—messy, caffeine-fueled, unfiltered, and fearless—thank you for not watering it down. Thank you for telling the truth in the ugliest, most beautiful way.

This book is a love letter to fire starters, soul survivors, and all the readers who don't just want the dark—they want to claim it.

Dedication JJ

Let's talk about how much love and support I have received from **Amber, Jacie,** and **Justice** when I was at a really low and dark place in my life. You three have filled me with so much joy and laughter— I can't even begin to express my appreciation for you, gals.

This book is where I finally got revenge on the men who have destroyed my mental health, made me the "monster" I am today. Someone who is hard to love, scared to love, but wants to be loved. Fuck you.

Most of all — Fuck you Darin. One day I will have justice... One day our daughter will have justice. You stripped me down to nothing, tried to rebuild me to fit your agenda. Tried to destroy me. I was more defiant than you bargained for but it did not warrant for you to beat me, drug me, and rearrange my thoughts to the point to where I feel like 10 years later, I would have been better off dead. Every "D" character you see, just know that's me taking my power back from you. You're the only person I can say I hate with my chest. I hope you have the days you deserve!

Trigger Warnings

This is a dark romantasy novel featuring mature themes, morally gray characters and intense emotional and physical content. Please read responsibly. Below is an exhaustive list of potential triggers present throughout the book.

Psychological & Emotional

Gaslighting & Manipulation

Intense verbal attacks

Humiliation & Degradation

Emotional Trauma

Depictions of dissociation

Panic attacks

Characters forced to relive painful memories

Dark Romance Tropes

Highly possessive, controlling MMC with Dominant and Aggressive tendencies

Forceful interactions including:

-Physical proximity without consent

-Intimidation through supernatural power

-Bonded mate trope with emotional coercion and resistance

Depiction of toxic emotional attachment that evolves

Themes of obsession, control, and protective rage

Violence & Gore

Brutal & Graphic scenes involving supernatural beings

Blood splatter, dismemberment, bone breaking and flesh tearing described in detail

Torture (psychological/physical)

On-page public execution (with emotional and visual impact)

Kill or be killed scenes

Death & Loss

On page death of characters

Death threats

Sexual & Related Themes

Multiple explicit sex scenes with dark intense emotional undertones

Powerplay during intimacy

Sexual tension rooted in hate to love, dominance and primal claiming

Aggressive, physical passion with minimal softness

Mentions of past sexual trauma (not detailed on page)

Mental Health

Ptsd, Depression, Grief, Thoughts of suicide

Other

Strong language, profanity, vulgar insults

Alcohol use

Scenes of confinement & captivity

Vengeance, rebellion, and inner darkness

This book is not intended for sensitive readers of those seeking light romance. If any of the above content may affect your mental health, please prioritize your safety and peace.

Chapter One

Nyxian

The Nobodies - Marilyn Manson

Y ou're such a beautiful fucking idiot.

A fucking whore, too—with your pathetic taste in men.

I stare down at her broken body, bloodied and twisted like a discarded doll. Skin split, bones misaligned, her breath rattling in a way that says she's not long for this world. And still—still—there's something delicate in the curve of her jaw, something infuriatingly soft in the way her lashes cling to the blood on her cheek.

It makes me sick.

Fragile.

Just like the rest of them.

Mortals always think they're invincible. That bad things only happen to *other* people. That they can chase thrill after thrill, dive headfirst into reckless nights, and come out unscathed.

Idiots.

I turn my attention to the wreckage. The car is mangled beyond recognition. It's a metallic corpse belching out smoke and fire. Flames snap at the edges of the hood like starving dogs, eager to consume what little is left. The tree they crashed into is still standing—scarred, sure, but unmoved. It's been here for centuries. Still rooted. Still unyielding.

The fire doesn't care. It lashes out like a tantrum-throwing child, furious that the world didn't bend to its chaos. Almost tragic. Almost funny.

Mostly, it's just pathetic.

Just another stupid mistake in a long list of mortal failures. I've seen it all before.

The driver's already gone. One of my brothers guided him into the Underworld like a dutiful little reaper. I didn't bother following. Drunken bastard got what he deserved.

But her?

She's still clinging.

Barely.

Blood trickles from her mouth as she tries to hold her chest together with trembling fingers. There's no time left for mortals to save her. Not that she'd deserve it. Her eyes snap to mine—wide, glassy, and brimming with fear. She knows. She *knows.*

She's not crying.

She should be.

She's not begging.

That's disappointing. I like it when they *beg.*

But she doesn't say a word. Doesn't scream. Doesn't plead. She just stares like she's trying to figure out *what* I am.

I mindlessly stare back. If I had eyes, I've took them. But I don't. So I give a figurative eye roll.

All I see is another mortal woman who made all the wrong choices.

Another fragile mortal who thought she was untouchable.

Why did you get in the car with him?

Why didn't you stay the fuck away from a drunk driver?

She's a breath away from death, and I *should* let her go.

But something twists. Something uncomfortable. Something I *don't* like.

I step closer. Her blood is everywhere now. It's slick and hot. It's painting the grass beneath her.

She *should've* died already.

And yet... *she clings*. Not to life. No, not really.

To *defiance*.

Interesting.

I crouch beside her, close enough to see the faint freckles hidden beneath the blood. She looks like the embodiment of fire—her hair, her rage, her energy. Even broken, she's burning.

"You really *are* a stupid bitch," I mutter. "But maybe not *just* a stupid bitch."

Her gaze sharpens. A flicker of something flares behind the fear.

There you are.

"You're dying," I whisper, leaning in so close she can feel the cold radiating off me. "*Beg* me to let you live."

Her lips part. "Help... me..." she coughs, spraying blood.

Pathetic.

"Just hold on, miss. We'll get you to the hospital."

The first responder's voice is sugar-sweet. Gentle. Reassuring.

What a fucking joke.

They lift her, broken and limp, onto the gurney. She whimpers, fingers twitching, and they start rolling her toward the ambulance. I trail behind them, slow and casual. I can't take her yet. Not until the clock above her head burns down to zero.

Red numbers float above her like a countdown from hell. Minutes left. Just fucking minutes.

Seconds ticking like a metronome set to her heartbeat.

Ambulance ride it is.

Maybe we'll stall at a crossing. Maybe a train will slice us all in half.

Her eyes keep darting from the paramedics to me, back and forth. Wide. Terrified. That's the look I like—when they realize *they're fucked*.

Another figurative eye roll.

They can't fucking see me, dumb bitch. Only you can.

I lean in again, whispering with the sweetness of poison. "You're dying."

Nearly seven hundred years of this shit. Picked by Exu himself to be a Reaper, trained in the dark arts of death delivery, and I *still* fucking hate it.

Same endless cycle. Same whimpering souls, same bleeding faces, same damn stories.

After I bag and tag Miss Wynne here, I'll be off to the next walking mistake—maybe some bastard who ate one too many double bacon cheeseburgers, or some wrinkled husk holding on by a thread and a tale from the "good ol' days."

Wynne, though...

She's gonna fight me. I can tell.

She's got that *look*.

That *burn* behind the fear.

So why not have a little fun?

Dangle a bargain. One she's too proud—or too dumb—to take.

I'm the embodiment of Death, but I sure as fuck don't look like the cartoons.

Mortals draw skeletons in cloaks. A Grim Reaper with a scythe and hollow eyes. Cute.

I'm worse.

I made sure of it.

Damn Azrael.

Always stepping into the spotlight like it was *made* for him.

I designed my form when I was angry—*agitated* beyond reason. I wasn't at peace like Exu told me to be. I wanted to *kill him*. I still might.

I was bred to be a soldier, not a fucking soul babysitter. But when Azrael started recruiting for his little army, I kept my name off the manifest just to spite him.

Because—*Fuck you, Azrael.*

Fuck you for being who you are.

Fuck you for being able to look at our father in the eyes like you weren't afraid.

And most of all...

Fuck you for being a reckless, chaotic little shit who *still* got a Fated Mate while I got this eternal shift on soul-duty.

I sigh as the ambulance screeches to a halt. First responders burst out, pulling Wynne inside like she's something to save.

She's not bad looking. For a mortal.

She's seen better days though—*literally.*

She flinches when the gurney bounces over the asphalt and barrels into the hospital. Her eyes are still locked on me. Not them. *Me.*

"Help... me..." she says again.

I walk beside her as if I belong. No one sees me. No one living can.

"*Beg*, Wynne," I murmur. "Maybe I'll cut you a deal."

My skull splits into a grin, all bone and malice.

"Please... help... me. Don't let me die. Please..." she chokes on blood.

Fucking disgusting bitch.

"I will spare you."

The words leave my mouth before I've fully decided if I mean them.

What could she possibly give me that I don't already own?

Power? Got it.

Souls? Please.

Freedom? That's a fucking joke.

But then it clicks—sharp and satisfying like a blade unsheathing.

Ah.

Yes.

That'll do.

"I'll spare you..." I say slowly, savoring the sound of it, "if you agree to save yourself—until I decide to claim you as mine."

Her breath catches.

She doesn't know what she's agreeing to.

Mortals never do.

She blinks up at the ceiling, what little life remains flickering in her eyes. The countdown above her is glowing red-hot now—three minutes, the seconds racing toward oblivion.

Will she say yes?

Will her pathetic, fragile heart *dare* to reach for survival?

"Yes... I will..." she whispers, and her eyes flutter shut as consciousness slips through her blood-stained fingers.

I grin. "Interesting," I murmur, clasping her hand in mine. My grip is cold, unforgiving.

The second our skin touches, the bargain seals.

A mark burns into her flesh—twisting, ancient, undeniable.

"M"—a sigil for *Marked*, etched in deep obsidian ink across her palm. A Reaper's contract... *My* contract.

Wynne...

You don't even understand what you've done.

You stupid, stupid bitch.

The countdown above her fades into nothing.

She no longer needs it.

I've given her immortality.

A curse dressed up as mercy.

She just doesn't know it yet.

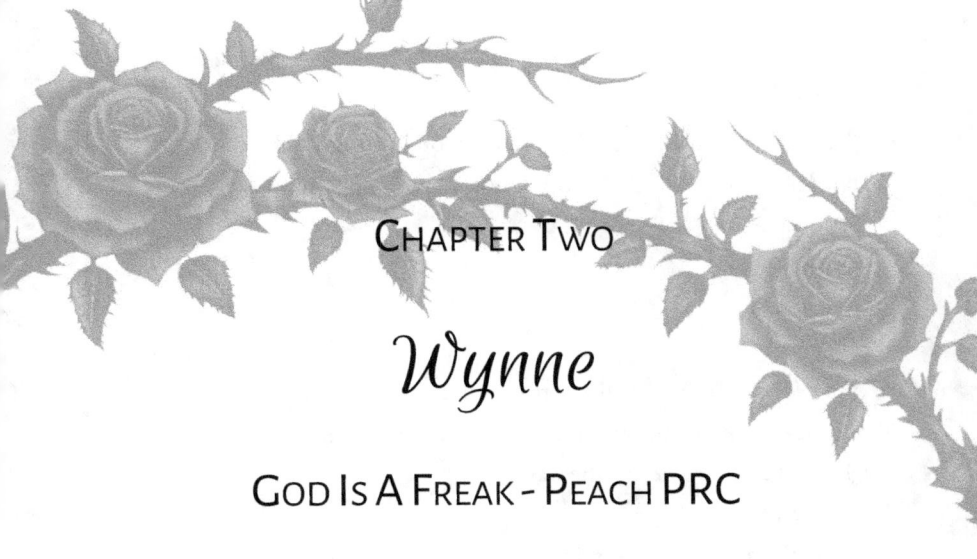

CHAPTER TWO

Wynne

GOD IS A FREAK - PEACH PRC

They said it was a miracle I walked out of that wreck alive.

Cole didn't.

Stupid, drunk asshole.

Nearly three years together, and I can't even squeeze out a single tear. Not one.

I'm not numb. That word doesn't even come close.

It's like the whole system meant for mourning got locked in some unreachable box inside me—and someone threw away the fucking key.

I exhale hard, trying to force the tension from my body.

Doesn't work.

I grab my phone off my desk instead. Working from home has its perks—mainly the ability to doom-scroll through everyone else's picture-perfect lives while mine sits in ruins.

Maybe I should sell everything and buy a fucking ranch.

Live like a goddamn prairie wife, barefoot and feral.

Wait—no. Animals. Gross. Too much poop. And I *hate* chickens.

I just need to *get out*. Out of this house. Out of my own head.

See people.

Dance.

Drink.

Have sex.

When's the last time I had an orgasm that wasn't self-inflicted?

A heatwave ripples through me before I can stop it—Cole's head between my thighs, his fingers inside me, the way he—

Nope. Not doing that.

I slam the mental brakes and yank open Facebook instead.

Let's see...

Friends list.

Who's attractive?

Single?

Has two functioning brain cells and wouldn't cry after bad sex?

I scroll. And scroll.

Ugh. Nothing.

How the hell do men make this look so easy?

They toss bait like it's a game—DM a dozen girls and wait for one to bite. All they want is a warm body and release.

Maybe I should try it.

I'm not looking for love. Just a damn distraction.

"Fuck!" I groan, slapping my laptop shut and pushing back from my desk.

This house smells like stale grief and loneliness.

I need something. Anything.

Maybe a drink.

Maybe a fuck.

Maybe...

A toy.

That's it!

That's the damned answer.

I type into Google: *"a fucking toy for women."*

Yep. My aggravation is bleeding through every keystroke.

Why are there *so many*?

Which one is best?

Why does this one have *seven* vibration speeds and that one only has *four*?

What does *suction mode* mean?

That one looks like a weapon.

That one has thirty thousand reviews—but half of them say it sucks?

What. The. Fuck.

I'm overwhelmed.

I slam the browser closed and faceplant into my bed, screaming into my pillow like the unhinged banshee I've apparently become.

"Fuck you, Cole," I mumble into the fabric. "For leaving me behind. For making me figure all this shit out alone. I don't know where to go from here. I don't know what the hell I'm doing."

Ding.

My phone buzzes.

I grope blindly for it, managing to knock it right off the nightstand.

"Bruh," I whisper into the void.

I roll onto my side, squinting at the glowing screen now mocking me from the floor.

"Come here, stupid," I grumble, snatching it up and unlocking it.

I swipe down to view my text notification.

Nadia:

> Wanna Party?

Well damn. Maybe there *is* a God.

I type back fast (maybe because I am scared she might change her mind):

Nadia:

Shit.

Wait!

Now I have to put pants on.

I groan dramatically and flop onto my back.

Large T-shirts and panties—that's my work-from-home uniform. The perks of remote life are *unmatched*.

The downside?

It takes me an eternity to get ready to actually go anywhere.

I haven't done laundry in *weeks*.

It takes another full week to fold it.

And a few more business days to finally put the shit away.

All to start the vicious cycle again.

But the real question is...

Do I have anything clean that screams "fuck me"?

To *any* gender at this point.

I just need a goddamn orgasm.

So any willing, consenting adult will do.

Preferably... a silver fox.

But beggars can't be choosers.

After rummaging through my closet like a raccoon on a caffeine high, I manage to find a pair of hot pink lace thongs and a pink glitter bodycon dress that barely—*barely*—covers the essentials.

If I bend over? God help us all.

But if it comes down to that?

Oh fucking well.

I glance in the mirror and do a full-body twirl.

Damn.

I look good.

Hot, actually.

Who wouldn't wanna bone me?

I grin at my reflection and blow myself a kiss, fully pleased with the outcome—even if I only had minutes to slap something together before some poor, pitiful soul hopefully ruins it all for me tonight.

Ruin me. *Please.*

I grab my purse off the closet door knob—pink, obviously—and head outside.

Nadia should be here soon.

A fire simmers in my belly, radiating full-on excitement.

I'm finally going out.

Finally hitting a party again.

The last time was...

Cole.

My stomach clenches.

How can I miss someone so stupid? So ignorant?

But he was beautiful.

And he had the tongue of a fucking god.

We were supposed to spend *forever* together.

Now it's just me.

Only me.

He's gone.

He fucking *abandoned* me when I begged him to call an Uber.

He didn't listen.

Didn't even *try* to stay alive.

That fucking asshole.

"*Ugh!*" I scream into the night sky.

I pace the porch like I'm waiting for my prom date to show up, but instead of a corsage, I want an orgasm and a shot of tequila. Preferably in that order. Or maybe reversed?

Fuck it. Dealer's choice.

I check my phone again.

Where the hell is Nadia?

Knowing her, she probably stopped for drive-thru tacos and forgot she was coming to get me. I wouldn't even be mad. Honestly, if she rolls up holding a Crunchwrap Supreme, I might cry and marry her on the spot.

My heels click on the porch, echoing into the quiet street like a desperate mating call.

Click-clack, *motherfuckers.*

Come get this slightly unstable, fully depressed, newly single woman in *heat.*

God, I sound like a walking red flag.

No—I *am* a walking red flag.

A glittery, bodycon-wrapped, emotionally-suppressed red flag with killer legs and rage issues.

Somewhere out there, a therapist is salivating at the thought of me.

I sink onto the porch step, carefully adjusting my dress to avoid flashing the neighborhood—although if Mr. Ramirez from next door wants a peek, I could use the ego boost.

I rest my elbows on my knees and stare out at the street, letting my thoughts simmer in the humidity.

Why does grief feel like wearing wet jeans?

Tight, heavy, uncomfortable, and you can't take them off without struggling and looking like a fool.

Everyone talks about moving on like it's this clean break, but it's not.

It's a slow rot.

You don't wake up one day and stop loving someone.

You just eventually stop looking for them in every room.

And still...

I do.

I look for him.

In shadows. In songs. In fucking memes.

"Ugh, Cole, you piece of shit," I mutter under my breath.

I stare up at the stars, imagining he's out there somewhere looking down at me, shaking his head at my hot pink thong.

Well, maybe he shouldn't have died and left me horny and unhinged.

I pull my phone out again, tempted to text my ex situationship from three years ago who moved to Idaho to start a potato farm or some shit.

But no.

I have *some* dignity left.

Besides, this night has potential.

Potential to be a disaster.

Potential to make mistakes that taste like cinnamon whiskey and regret.

I just need to *feel* something again.

Even if it's temporary.

Even if I wake up tomorrow with smeared eyeliner and the crushing realization that nothing's changed.

That's future Wynne's problem.

Current Wynne?

She's ready to sweat, scream, and sin her way through the night.

Headlights flash at the end of the block.

A beat-up Jeep with a pink air freshener swinging from the mirror comes into view.

"Thank *God*," I exhale, standing and brushing off my thighs.

Let the chaos begin.

Chapter Three

Wynne

SLUT! - Bea Miller

Music pulses through my veins, vibrating every inch of my body. Bodies grind against me, a wild sea of flesh in perfect chaos. It's a fucking *rush*. The sweat, the heat, the thumping bass that drowns out everything but the desperate need clawing at me from the inside.

It's my escape—my salvation—my fucking exhale. In this godforsaken club, I can pretend none of it matters. The wreck. Cole's death. Losing him. All of it is far from my mind as my body moves like it's not even mine.

But that craving—that *need*—the one that's always there, gnawing at me in the quiet moments, the one I can't chase away? It's not satisfied by the music, not by the strangers' sweat-slicked skin rubbing up against mine. No. I need more friction—*real* friction. Friction I can't give myself.

A man brushes against me, tall, freckled, and the kind of redhead who doesn't make me feel like an outcast for once. His muscles ripple as he leans into me, his bicep straining beneath his shirt. *God, those fucking arms.* They'd look so fucking good holding my neck, keeping me in place while he takes me from behind.

My mouth goes dry.

Whatever pill he slipped me, it's working wonders. My body feels like it's vibrating on a different frequency, calm but fucking buzzing, every cell in me begging to be released. I'm so wound up I'm about to snap in half.

I glance up at him. This red-headed beauty. My eyes trace the sharp planes of his face, his hungry stare locked onto me like I'm the only thing in this room worth looking at.

Hunger. *Hunger for me.*

I need this. I need him. I press my tits into him, just enough to feel the pressure against my skin, just enough to remind him that I'm fucking *alive* and he's the one who's about to feel the burn.

What the hell is his name again?

Tom? Jerry? No, that's the cartoon running rampant in my mind. *Jones?* Nah. *Dave?* No. *Damian?*

Darin.

His name is *Darin.*

He leans in, and I can smell it—cheap men's cologne—cloying and overpowering. Normally, that would make me recoil, but not tonight. Tonight, I'm a fucking animal. A wild, untamed beast, rubbing against anything I can find for that one hit of satisfaction like a fucking cat in heat.

Why the hell am I even stressing about a name? What's it matter? It's not like I'm going to call him in the middle of the night, asking for more. I don't need another fuckboy to add to the roster of mistakes. Not right now.

"Wanna get out of here?" he yells over the roar of the music. His voice is thick with need, almost comical, but there's that glint in his eyes that say he's not joking.

It's the mating call, that line they all memorize—probably from some rom-com they binge while playing with their balls in their moms' basements. Still, it works. And for once, I don't mind being the prey.

I give him a look, a half-smirk, my teeth flashing for a split second, *daring* him to make his move. "Lead the way," I murmur.

I smirk, accepting his bold offer with a flick of my wrist. His words are the kind of bold that could either satisfy us both for the night or leave us both aching for more by morning. One of us will walk away pleased, and I know damn well it won't be me. Not unless he's one of those "*nice guys*," the ones that are overrated in every other situation *but* under the sheets. The kind that aim to please, but with a dominant edge that drives me to the fucking brink.

I wouldn't even mind if he was a pushover outside of the bedroom, as long as he knew how to take charge in the right moments. And god, does he need to know how to dance under the covers.

He grabs my hand, pulling me through the crowd. I glance back at Nadia, sending her a knowing smile. This isn't a rescue mission. I'm more than willing, and when I get back, I'll give her every *single* dirty detail.

The music begins to fade as we step further into the night, his hand still firmly gripping mine, dragging me through the thumping bass and colorful lights toward the parking lot. And that's when I see it. *That car.*

What the fuck?

A Mustang. A convertible. A fucking red one.

Seriously? Does every man think this is some kind of "babe magnet?" It's like a neon sign shouting, *Look at me, I'm compensating for something!*

I'm car stupid, sure, but even I know a Mustang is a walking advertisement for tiny dick syndrome. But hell, I'm desperate enough tonight to try it out, maybe pretend I like it if it gets me to my goal. Maybe it'll be enough to coax at least a *mini* orgasm out of this farce.

We tumble into the back seat, clothes flying off in a chaotic rush. I don't even get the chance to catch my breath before he's already skipping the foreplay, straight into whatever the fuck this is. A wet, sloppy sound fills the air, and then—yep—he's already inside me.

I roll my eyes on the inside, closing them on the outside. I pray to whatever sex gods might be listening, hoping that this lasts long enough to put a dent in the beast raging inside me. A few minutes—*please,* just a few minutes.

And then I hear it.

"Whore."

What the fuck?

I open my eyes, squinting up at him. "Did you say something?"

Darin doesn't respond at first, too lost in his own rhythm. "No," he groans, but the voice—that voice—doesn't match his.

It's not his voice. It's deep, guttural, like the growl of someone who's been holding onto their anger for too long.

I don't get a chance to process that because Darin is too busy with his *own* rhythm, thrusting into me like it's the last time he'll ever get the chance.

One thrust. Two thrusts. Three. Four.

It's not enough.

I'm hoping for something, anything, to push me over the edge, but instead, I'm left to count the beats in my head, waiting for something to happen. But just as the familiar burn starts to creep up my spine, Darin stops. Just... stops.

"Goddammit!" I mutter under my breath.

No, his name is *Darin*—not David, not Darrell. What the fuck is going on tonight?

Something wet hits my neck—cold, sticky. My first instinct is disgust. Did this asshole just spit on me?

I blink my eyes open, the sensation of his breath still fresh on my skin. But then, I freeze.

Darin's once hungry eyes are now wide and vacant, like hollow pits staring into nothingness. His lips are parted, and that's when I see it—the blood. Thick, dark red fluid pouring from his mouth, pooling on my chest and dripping onto the leather seats of the mustang. It's not just blood. It's... wrong. It's as if his very life is spilling out of him, staining everything he touches.

"What the fuck, asshole?" I manage to choke out, my voice hoarse, the words barely forming in my throat as panic claws at me.

I fumble for the car light, my hands shaking violently, slapping against the button until it finally clicks on.

And then I scream.

The shrill, terrified sound rips from my throat as I see what's become of him. His throat is caved in, collapsed like a crushed can. Blood floods from the gaping wound in his neck, rushing out like a river, staining everything around us. His body feels unnaturally heavy as I shove him off me, the dead weight pulling me down with him. His once muscular form is now slack and lifeless. My heart pounds in my ears, my stomach turning over violently.

I scramble, desperate to free myself from the scene, from the suffocating weight of the mustang, the overwhelming, suffocating smell of blood. The car is closing in on me, too small, too confining. His body feels like it's made of stone, not flesh.

I rip my dress and shoes free, my hands slick with blood, my breath ragged and erratic. I push myself out of the car, stumbling to the ground. The cool air slaps me in the face, but it's not enough to clear my head. I need to get out. I need to—

I freeze.

Something's watching me.

Before I can even make sense of it, Nadia's there, her voice sharp, panic in her tone.

"Wynne? Are you okay? What's going on?"

I turn to her, but my vision is blurry, my mind a jumbled mess of terror. My chest heaves as I try to catch my breath. Her words seem muffled, distant. I can barely focus on her face, her concern. All I can see are Darin's empty eyes, his blood, and the heavy silence that now surrounds us.

But there's something else.

The air feels... wrong.

I look around, the shadows of the parking lot stretching unnaturally, bending in ways they shouldn't. The darkness feels deeper than it should be, like it's alive, crawling towards me, closing in on us.

I force my legs to move, but I can't stop shaking. My mind is racing, but every thought is lost in the chaos of fear that consumes me. And then—then I hear it.

A low, guttural sound from the direction of the mustang. Not a human sound, but something... else. Something that shouldn't be.

CHAPTER FOUR

Nyxian

I WANNA BE YOUR SLAVE - MANESKIN

I didn't explain myself very well, *apparently*. It's not about jealousy, but I refuse to share what's mine. And Wynne, you *belong* to me. Your soul, life, your fucking body– your god damn essence. Everything about you.. *I own*.

The poor fool didn't see it coming. How pathetic is it to be caught in such a way—trapped in his own car seat while he tries to satiate some twisted desire. I'm not concerned about the consequences. The bargain is in place, and the Keres are already on their way to collect his soul and ravage what's left behind.

It's for the best. I'll need to be careful, though. Persuading mortals and helping Wynne to avoid the mortal laws will be tricky, but it's worth the effort. She's mine to guide, to protect, to claim. I've been keeping an eye on her. I know what she's been looking at, even what she's considering. It's... almost amusing.

Earlier, I noticed her curiosity. Vibrators. Dildos. It wasn't the first time, and it certainly won't be the last. I've taken it upon myself to gift her a collection—something I've placed on her bed, waiting for her return. Thirty-two, to be exact. Some are for me, too, when the time comes to show her exactly what I want to do to her.

She's not ready yet. But soon, she will be. There are things I need to teach her. It's been a long time since I've had a female—centuries, in fact. Wynne will be my first mortal, however. She's a helpless romantic, unaware of how much she *will* need me. How much she'll crave me when I'm finished. I've even been practicing my mortal form, trying to perfect the way I hold her. It's something the shadows assist with, keeping me in control.

I've grown used to solitude, to being alone. But this hunger... it gnaws at me. It's been far too long since I've allowed myself to indulge in something more. This bargain with Wynne—it's an *experiment*. A way to prove that I don't have to remain solitary. Maybe, just maybe, it will give me an inkling of the happiness I've denied myself for so long.

Why should others like Azrael be granted such things—a Fated Mate, no less—while I work relentlessly, with no one to come home to? I deserve to have someone. To have a place to return to. Someone who will cook for me, someone who will see the value in the work I do. But more than that, someone who will give me the release I need. Someone who will... *understand*.

I look at Wynne, her face smeared with blood. It's a jarring contrast to her pale skin, but it only makes her blue eyes stand out more. Her hair is wild, messy—like flames that frame her face. For a moment, I can't help but wonder how she would look beneath me, with all her delicate features laid bare. What would she look like with my cum covering her body?

What color are my mortal eyes, anyway? I've never bothered to look in a mirror in my mortal form. It feels vain, unnecessary. Would she even find my mortal form attractive?

I sigh, letting the thoughts drift away.

She doesn't have a choice, just as I didn't have one when I was forced into this existence. She belongs to me now. I've made sure of it. I tricked her into this—my little fucking bargain—and I won't apologize.

Maybe, just maybe, I'll feel a little guilty, but not enough to change anything. I can't. *She's mine.*

I'm looking at the bright side, at least. She'll be here. Someone to talk to—even if she can never truly understand the weight of what I am, what I've become. She'll be there for me in the ways I need her to be. And, yes, she'll be mine, for the rest of *our* immortal life.

I pull up her friend's expiration date. Nadia. Three weeks. Thirty-six hours. Twelve minutes. The seconds are ticking away.

Nadia Jones. A lifelong resident of Picayune. How the hell did I end up in this *insignificant* little town?

I glance over her file, pondering. Not a bad-looking girl. But what interests me more is her yellow complexion against the stark neon pink of her hair. It's like a puzzle I haven't figured out yet. A dragon tattoo across her back... fucking why?

What really irks me, though, is that hideous cheetah print dress. And when she bends over, it's as if she's begging for attention, giving everything away.

Then there's Wynne—so innocent, so bright, wrapped in pink from head to toe, down to her nails. What the hell did I get myself into?

But Wynne? She's not the same as the others. She's different. She has that *spark*, that fire that both *irritates* and *excites* me. She'll fight me at every turn, and I'll *enjoy* it—every second of it. She thinks she's clever, that she's in control, but that's the beauty of it. She doesn't even realize how badly she's already lost.

She'll try to fight it, I know that. She'll resist me because it's in her nature to do so. She'll test me, push my buttons, and that's fine. I like it that way. The harder she fights, the harder I'll *break* her, and that's when I'll really begin to enjoy myself.

I've spent too long in this existence to let anything slip through my fingers. And Wynne? She's mine. Every part of her is mine, whether she likes it or not. She'll come to me eventually, I know it. I'll make her.

And when she does... when she gives in to me, I'll have everything I've ever wanted. She'll be the one who finally makes me feel something real, something more than this hollow existence of mine.

I don't care if I have to be cruel to make her see it. Sometimes, cruelty is the only thing that gets through to mortals. And if that's what it takes to make her understand how much she belongs to me, then so be it.

I'm not jealous. I'm not possessive, not in the way most people think. No. I simply refuse to share what's mine. And Wynne? She's fucking mine!

And it'll be my pleasure to make her realize that, every single day of her life.

CHAPTER FIVE

Wynne

I don't even know how to explain what the fuck just happened to that guy. I'm now plagued with nightmares— flashbacks of blood, his caved in throat. Thankfully, he had a dash cam. Embarrassing I know, but it was able to prove I'm not a fucking cold-blooded killer.

Nadia, being the sweet (and probably highly regretting) friend she is, drove me home. We said our farewells, and now I'm standing in front of my door, clutching a handful of keys like a goddamn fool, covered in blood. How have I lived here for years and still can't remember which one of these stupid keys opens the door? It's like some twisted game of *which one doesn't belong* every time I walk up to the damn thing.

I let out a sigh and bang my forehead against the door, feeling the cool wood against my skin. I almost scream—seriously, it's just been one of those days—but I swallow it, biting down hard on the urge. The sting of tears hits my eyes, and before I can stop it, they start falling. I don't even care. This is the tipping point, the breaking point where I'm *beyond* sexually frustrated, mentally drained, and I'm pretty sure I'm on the verge of full-blown depression.

Why the hell does life feel like it's coming at me in waves of dumb and frustration? Like, who even signed me up for this ridiculous rollercoaster?

With one final, defeated exhale, I twist the doorknob—please, humor me, give me a break. Tell me I didn't lock the door...

Lo and behold, I didn't lock the damn door.

Thank. Fucking. God.

I step inside, toe my shoes off like a grumpy toddler, and fling my purse to the ground, completely disregarding my grandmother's warning about how "your purse should never touch the floor if you don't want to be broke."

Fuck that, I think, shaking my head. I'll be broke if I want to. I'm tired, I'm pissed, and honestly, I need a goddamn break from everything. If that's what it takes, then I'll take my chances.

I wander down the hallway, my frustration growing with every step as I make my way to my room. I flick the lights on in a fit of anger and—what the hell?

Wait.

What?

Did I forget I ordered these? Because there's no way this many boxes just appeared on my bed while I was gone. I'm pretty sure I remember walking out this morning and seeing nothing but a regular, boring old bed. And now? Now, there are *a ton* of boxes.

I pause, staring at the pile of them like a deer caught in headlights. Did someone break in and leave a joke at my expense?

What kind of sick prank is this? Is someone playing with my life right now? Is this some kind of twisted way to remind me how *alone* I am?

I grab the first box, ripping into it with all the grace of a frustrated, emotionally drained woman on the brink of snapping.

A tentacle dildo.

Wait, what?

Is this a joke? Did someone decide that my life needed to be spiced up with the most bizarre, WTF package ever?

I blink a few times, trying to process what's happening. No. No way. This can't be real. What the hell kind of sicko buys *this* for me? But then again, considering what just happened with Damian (or was it David? Who even knows anymore), I'm starting to question my own sanity.

I keep going, ripping open more boxes, my eyes growing wider as the contents become even more absurd. Some vibrate. Some suck. Some have suction cups that I'm not sure what kind of "science experiment" they were designed for.

Is this what my life is now? Am I really *this* sexually deprived that someone out there is throwing thirty-two—yes, thirty-two—sex toys at me like I'm some sort of... sex toy enthusiast?

I can't help but laugh, although it's more of a desperate, "what the actual fuck is going on?" laugh.

Who even needs thirty-two sex toys?

Who's trying to tell me something?

I grab a dildo, this one shaped like a dragon (don't ask me why), and inspect it like I'm studying for some kind of demented exam. I turn it over in my hands and have to stop myself from just rolling my eyes so hard they might get stuck in the back of my head.

This is just... *ridiculous.*

Bro, what. The. Fuck. Is. Going. On?

I throw my hands up in frustration, standing in my room surrounded by boxes, all of them mocking me with their very existence. What kind of life is this? Honestly. It's like I'm living in a parody of my own existence, but there's no punchline to make it funny.

Nope. Just thirty-two dildos.

Maybe tomorrow I'll have a breakdown over this. Or maybe I'll just start a new hobby. But for now? For now, I'm going to shower and then sit on my bed, surrounded by a mountain of ridiculous sex toys, and try to figure out how to keep my sanity intact.

I start moving the boxes into the closet—except for one small black vibrator that claims to be purse-sized. I laugh. Who carries a vibrator around with them wherever they go?

You know what? That actually might come in handy.

I open the box and start fiddling with the buttons. The vibration is surprisingly intense, even just on my hand, and a curious anticipation builds. God, I'm so sexually frustrated. I've never needed a release more in my life.

I kick off my dress, tossing it to the side along with my thong, and climb into the shower really quick and then retreat to my bed. The little device feels almost comforting as I test it. The hum against my skin sends a ripple of pleasure through me, the sensation soothing some of the tension I've been carrying for too long.

Chapter Six

Nyxian

Monster - Meg Myers

I knew she'd enjoy at least one of them. Even if she pretended to be confused, the curiosity always wins out. She doesn't have patience—doesn't know the first damn thing about it—and lucky for her, I'm an exceptional teacher.

She'll learn.

My way.

I watch her from the shadowed corner of her room, hidden just outside the range of mortal perception. Her soft whimpers float through the space, followed by the quiet hum of the toy. She's squirming, shifting, trying to reach that edge she's too tightly wound to fall over. That *desperation*... it's *delicious*.

She finally gives up, collapsing back onto the bed with a sigh and a frustrated stare at the ceiling. Poor thing. She needs to be fucked properly, ruined the right way—*my* way—but we're not there yet. *She's* not there yet.

Then she grabs her phone.

I move closer, silently, drawn by the sugary bubblegum scent of her perfume mixed with arousal. I lean in and inhale, letting it coat my senses, trying not to lose myself in the intoxicating sweetness.

She scrolls through her contacts and pauses on a name: **Ryan.**

Ryan.

My jaw tenses.

Bold. She's testing limits she doesn't even realize exist. I watch her thumbs move across the screen:

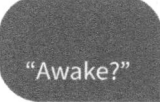

His reply is immediate.

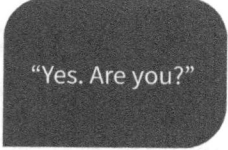

Clearly, genius. She messaged first.

Imaginary eye roll.

Then she types:

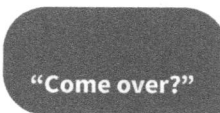

And the fool responds without hesitation:

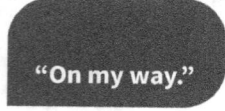

Of course he is. Another idiot with a dick and a dream, thinking he's about to get lucky. Thinking *she's* available.

I step back into the shadows, arms crossed as I settle into the corner with a full view. Let her think she's got control. Let her think this is her idea. It's more fun when they realize how little choice they ever had.

She gets up, butt naked, as if she hasn't just summoned her own funeral. I follow her with my eyes, watching the hypnotic sway of her hips and her ass jiggling as she heads to the bathroom.

I trail after her, invisible but ever-present.

She turns on the shower, humming some off-key mortal tune that makes my ears twitch. I don't recognize the song and I don't care. It's probably one of those emotion-drenched, overproduced disasters mortals love to blare while pretending they're healing. Or sulking. Or whatever it is they do.

She steps into the water, and the scent of arousal fades slowly as she scrubs herself raw. I watch every motion—the glide of her hands across her skin, the way her breath hitches when the water turns too hot. She lathers her hair, then grabs a razor, dragging it down her legs with practiced ease.

She's trying. Trying to clean herself, to prepare herself. *For him.*

Disrespectful!

She finishes, wrapping herself in a fluffy pink towel, and pads back to the vanity like she's not about to make the biggest mistake of her life. The blow dryer roars to life. Her hair flutters around her like flame, chaotic and beautiful. Her blue eyes are focused, but her mouth holds a slight pout of dissatisfaction. She doesn't *really* want Ryan. She just wants to feel *wanted.*

I could give her that. I could give her so much more.

But she doesn't deserve it yet.

She doesn't deserve *me* yet.

Let her get dressed. Let him knock on the door. Let her answer it with that fake smile and practiced innocence. I'll be watching every second. I want her to feel the tension in her spine, the chill across her skin. I want her to wonder if she's being watched.

Because she is.

She always will be.

And when she finally learns her place?

She'll *beg for me.*

31

She rummages through her dresser like she isn't under surveillance, completely unaware that every little movement is driving me closer to the edge. She pulls out a matching pink bra and panty set, soft lace and delicate straps, like temptation tailored just for me. She even adds the thigh-high pink socks.

Of course.

Everything about her is fucking pink.

Why is *everything* in this room pink?

The bedding. The curtains. The damn lamp. Even the little rug by her bed.

It's cute.

It's infuriating.

Because it's *hers*. And she's about to hand all that softness over to *him*.

Jealousy coils through my chest, spreading heat down my spine, lighting every bone in my body on fire. My fists clench, teeth grinding.

Then the fucking doorbell rings.

She starts walking, and I swear to the gods, I almost lose it.

That ass.

Jiggling with every... single... fucking... step.

Fuck.

I follow her through the house, barely containing the storm roiling inside me. Every breath I take is thick with her scent—sugar, sex, and shampoo. She smells like sin and softness, and she's about to give it away to a man who hasn't earned it.

She opens the door.

And it's worse than I imagined.

He's scrawny. A twig in a too-tight black t-shirt, with greasy hair and a hard-on forming just from looking at her. His brown eyes drag over her body like he's already unwrapping her.

I damn near *kill him* on the spot.

But no—death would be too easy. She needs to learn.

She needs to *understand*.

"Hey, Ryan," she says, soft and sheepish, like she's unsure.

Good. Be unsure! You should be.

He smirks, clearly mistaking her nervousness for desire. "Hello, Wynne," he says, stepping inside and closing the door like he belongs here.

He doesn't.

His hand runs down her arm, lingering far too long. Then he moves to her waist, her side, her gods damned chest. He palms her breast and she lets out a sound—half a moan, half resignation.

I freeze, my own breath caught in my throat.

I hate this.

I hate *him*.

And worse... I hate that she's fucking letting it happen.

An ache blooms in my chest. The kind that makes rational thought vanish. The kind that has me teetering on the edge of revealing everything. But I stop myself.

Wait. Just wait, Nyxian.

I follow them back into her bedroom. She lets him touch her. Kiss her. Press her into the mattress like he's earned the right to be here. Their lips crash. Moans mix. He fumbles with his belt while she shimmies out of her panties.

I watch as a phantom in the corner, unseen but all-seeing. Ryan drops his boxers, revealing what I can only describe as disappointing.

That's it?

I chuckle quietly, the sound lost in the slapping of lips and the rustle of sheets. Maybe I *should* let this happen. Maybe I should let her remember this when I finally take her and *ruin* her.

Because she has no idea what real satisfaction feels like.

He mounts her in a rush, skipping everything she needs—foreplay, attention, worship. She moans, but it's forced. Overdone. She's faking it, and badly. He doesn't notice. Of course he doesn't. His ego is already inflating.

He flips her over. She gets on all fours. Her perfect ass arches into the air.

And my restraint dies.

That ass...

Bouncing with every pathetic thrust.

I clench my jaw so hard I think I might break it. That's *mine*. All of her is *mine*. And watching this joke of a man grind into her like a goddamn amateur?

No.

Absolutely fucking not.

I raise a hand and snap my fingers once.

Ryan gasps, clutching his chest. His knees buckle. He collapses off of her like a ragdoll, thudding to the floor. Wynne is still for a beat, breath caught, blinking in confusion.

She glances over her shoulder, then down at him.

Then, slowly, her wide eyes lift—

Right to where I'm standing now.

Visible. Towering. Unapologetic.

I smile.

Cold. Wicked. Possessive.

"Lesson one," I murmur, voice laced with venom and promise. "You don't let *anyone* touch what belongs to me."

I take a deep breath, trying to gather myself once more.

"Hello, Wynne," I whisper.

She jolts like she's been electrocuted, scrambling back across the bed. The pink blanket barely covers her, and the panic in her eyes shifts between me and the wheezing mess on the floor.

Good. Let her panic. Let her *feel* me now.

I stroll toward them, calm and slow, savoring the fear dripping off her like perfume. I crouch beside Ryan, who's still curled up and clutching his chest like he's got a hope in hell of surviving this night.

I tilt my head, examining him with a detached curiosity. "I was going to let you fuck my girl," I say, my voice silk and steel. "Let you get your little moment of glory. But then you skipped the most *important* part of sex."

I hum thoughtfully, as if this is just a casual conversation between friends and not his last few breaths.

"Foreplay, Romeo. You skipped *foreplay*."

Ryan wheezes. Pathetic.

"How inconsiderate can you be?" I continue, leaning closer. "Especially when you're only working with..." I glance down at this limp dick, the little disappointment between his legs, letting my lip curl in amusement. "What's that? Maybe four and a half inches? On a *good* day?"

I cluck my tongue.

Wynne gasps, covering her mouth, mortified—but still watching me. *Always* watching me now.

"I mean, you came in swinging with a butterknife and expected to carve up a steak." I smirk, eyes locked on hers now. "I don't share my food, sweetheart. And I *definitely* don't let anyone leave crumbs on my plate."

CHAPTER SEVEN

Wynne

SLUT! - BEA MILLER

I can't even put into words what the actual fuck is happening right now.

My eyes ping-pong between Ryan—who is now laid out on my floor like he just failed a gym class fitness test—and the *thing* standing in the middle of my damn bedroom.

Like... what the fuck even *is* that?

A tall skeleton cloaked in a black robe like he just walked out of Hot Topic's exclusive Grim Reaper line. His teeth are unnervingly sharp, like shark-level sharp. And there's this faint, eerie glow around him—dark blood red, like fresh pomegranate juice, but make it demonic.

And then he looks at me.

My breath just full-on nopes out of my body.

"You don't need to cover up," the thing says, voice so deep and sinful it might be illegal in some states. "I've already watched you shower. We're past the shy phase, my dear."

Excuse me, *what*?

I shake my head violently. Nope. This isn't happening. I am clearly having a stress-induced hallucination. I've finally snapped. I've officially gone off the deep end and landed in pervert hell. And to top it all off? I *still* find the voice attractive.

What the fuck is wrong with me?

This is some messed up romance novel plotline Nadia would shove in my hands while whispering, *"It's morally gray, babe, just go with it."*

And I'd be like, "No, Nadia, she's being kidnapped!"

And now here I am... aroused by Skeletor with a six-pack.

"This isn't real," I whisper to myself, squeezing my eyes shut. "This isn't real. This is the tentacle dildo coming back to haunt me."

But then I feel his breath—cold and ghostly—brush across my ear.

"I am as real as the urge you have to get fucked," he murmurs.

Waterfall.

I feel it. Between my legs. Like some pathetic Pavlovian response.

Oh my God.

I'm not okay.

Reluctantly, I open my eyes. Ryan's wheezing has gone silent, which is both suspicious and oddly relieving. Now all I hear is the faint sound of breathing—*his* breathing—right beside me.

"I'm Nyxian," he says, like that's supposed to mean anything to me.

He steps back slightly, giving me a full view of his shadow-wrapped form. Shadows curl off him like smoke. I swear they're reaching for me—wrapping around my ankles like curious cats.

"I—" My voice cracks. "What... what are you?"

He tilts his head like he's amused. "Do you remember?"

"Remember what?" I somehow force out, even though my entire body has decided to become a statue.

"Our *bargain*." He sounds almost nostalgic, like we shared coffee and trauma once. "I didn't claim your soul because you made a..." He pauses, like the right

38

word is stuck on the tip of his monstrous tongue. "*Promise*. You made a promise to me in exchange for your life."

And just like that—*bam*.

A flash.

A memory so quick and sharp it's like being stabbed with a photo. The hospital. Blood. Screaming. My own voice, promising something—*anything*—just to live.

Holy. Shit.

"I've seen you before," I murmur.

He grins. And it's not cute. It's not warm. It's sharp, wicked, and *absolutely* the smile of a creature who'd enjoy watching you squirm.

"I'm not here to hurt you, Wynne." His smile widens. "I'm only here to remind you what you owe me."

My mouth is drier than my love life. I try to speak but all I manage is a weird frog noise.

"What... do you want from me?" I finally ask.

He leans back, those shadows twitching at his feet like they're excited. "I'm tired of watching you be a *whore*," he hisses.

I blink.

I blink again.

"*Excuse me?*"

Did Mr. Sexy Skeleton just slut-shame me in my own house?

Sir, I may be underdressed and over-lubricated, but I *will* throw hands.

"You promised me that you would wait for me," he growls, voice like velvet-lined thunder, "and not do stupid shit like *this*."

He waves his hand toward Ryan, whose limp body is still lying on the floor like a glitch in my personal horror movie.

"Why are you doing this to me?!" I scream, the panic cracking through my chest like a sledgehammer.

Nyxian doesn't flinch. He just keeps walking, slow and deliberate, stepping right over Ryan's motionless form until he's standing at the foot of my bed—like death incarnate on a personal mission to destroy any remaining sanity I might have had.

"A promise," he says, voice dangerously calm, "*is a promise.*"

He lifts his chin slightly, eyes—well, sockets—locked on me. "Your life and right to breathe in return... you are to be my mate."

"...Mate?" I bark the word out, confusion and rage all tangled in my throat. "*Mate?!*"

He shrugs one shoulder with infuriating nonchalance. "How do you mortals say it... marriage?"

Then the fucker throws in air quotes. "You accepted my bargain. So you're now my '*wife*.'"

My mouth opens. Closes. My brain pulls the fire alarm, and still—nothing.

I just stare at him, eyes burning as hot as my cheeks, and now my tears are falling like some kind of cosmic joke.

I don't get it.

I *don't understand what the hell is happening.*

And to top it all off?

The ache between my thighs comes back with a vengeance.

Oh my God. No.

Not now.

Not while Skeletor from the Lust Dimension is claiming marriage rights and disposing of failed Tinder hookups like it's part of his weekend routine.

What kind of reverse romance novel hell is this?

Nadia is going to *lose her mind* if I ever tell her about this.

Nyxian leans forward, planting both hands on the bed like some dark deity ready to consume my soul—and honestly? That might not be the worst part of my day.

"Go to sleep," he whispers, his voice curling around me like smoke. "I will take care of the body."

My lips part. I want to scream. I want to demand answers. I want to *fucking punch him in the teeth.*

But I don't move.

I don't speak.

"You don't deserve to get *fucked* tonight," he adds, cold and final, as if that's some kind of divine punishment.

And that?

That *really* pisses me off.

But I can't fight it.

I'm numb. I'm tired. I'm still soaking wet and humiliated.

I lie back, pulling the blanket tighter around myself like it could shield me from everything I've just seen... just felt.

This isn't real.

It *can't* be real.

If I just sleep... maybe this nightmare will reset. Maybe I'll wake up, and Ryan will still be trying to figure out where the clit is, and Nyxian will be nothing more than a sex-deprived hallucination.

So I listen.

Because what the fuck else can I do?

This.

Isn't.

Fucking.

Real.

Chapter Eight

Wynne

Dirty Dirty - Charlotte Cardin

The fact that I wake up in the middle of the fucking woods tells me two things.

One: maybe it wasn't a dream.

Two: maybe my subconscious just felt guilty about the emotional trauma and decided to throw in a scenic upgrade.

Trees tower above me like they're silently judging every one of my life choices, which is fair, because I'm in a *sheer pink nightgown* and I'm *barefoot*. Not cute forest fairy barefoot. No. I'm more *unhinged sleepwalker Barbie lost in the woods* barefoot.

There's a rustling somewhere to my left. I spin around so fast I nearly flash the damn trees some tits. Nothing. Just branches. Wind. Silence.

I look down at my ridiculous outfit again. See-through. *Pink.* No underwear.

My subconscious is either a sadist... or Nyxian personally curated this outfit to piss me off.

I wander deeper into the trees, no idea where I'm going, no idea why I'm not waking up yet.

"Run, Wynne."

His voice slices through the stillness like a blade across silk. I freeze.

Where is he?

"*I said fucking run.*"

This time, he steps out from behind a tree, all towering shadows and spiteful smirks. "I bet my shadows can catch you—since you love fucking mind games so much."

The ground shifts beneath me. Tendrils of darkness shoot out like cracked whips, slithering around my ankles.

I scream, kicking at them, teeth gritted, pure adrenaline. "*Get off!*"

I break free and bolt.

Branches claw at my skin, shadows swipe at my arms like angry hands, but I keep going. I don't know where. I don't know *why*.

I just *know* I don't want to be caught.

I need to wake up.

I *have* to wake up.

"I'm about to give you a teaser of what you asked for, Little Disaster," his voice echoes through the trees. "Don't let me catch you. Might be hard for me to stop..."

I run harder. My breath comes in shallow, panicked bursts. The forest twists and warps around me. Is this even real? Why the fuck does it *feel* real?

I glance over my shoulder.

Bad idea.

A shadow comes out of nowhere and *clotheslines* me.

I slam to the ground so hard the breath punches out of my lungs.

I scream. "*Get away from me!*"

Shadows crawl up my legs, wrap around my wrists, pulling, *tugging*, pinning me to the forest floor like they *own* me.

And then—he steps out of the shadows.

Not the skeletal version.

Not the cloaked horror from last night.

Flesh.

And *fuck* me.

Jet black hair, tousled like he's just rolled out of a storm.

Skin the color of sun-drenched bronze.

Dark eyes that look like they could rip through souls and still somehow make you *wet*.

He's tall, but not monstrous. Broad. Built. Muscles trace down his chest and forearms like living art. Not bodybuilder big. More like... fighter. *Lethal. Beautiful.*

My legs are still spread. The shadows still have me. But now I just... *stop.*

I stop kicking. I stop screaming.

My brain short-circuits.

Because I know this has to be a dream, and honestly?

If this is the only way I'm getting laid this year, then my dignity can wait.

I lower my gaze in defeat. My body goes slack, trembling, the sheer fabric of the nightgown fluttering in the breeze like a joke at my expense.

This is a dream.

It *has* to be.

Because in dreams, even when you want to fight, even when your gut says run...

You *never* win.

This is just my subconscious playing a sick joke on me.

A fever dream brought on by unchecked sexual frustration.

Because for fuck's sake—I need *something.*

Anything.

A damn *orgasm,* a single flicker of relief. I don't care if it's a ghostly tongue in the dark or just five seconds of someone's mouth between my legs—I'm desperate. Pathetic. And apparently, my brain knows it.

"You're such a bad girl, Wynne," his voice croons like a lullaby laced in sin. "A disaster running amok. What *am* I going to do with you?"

I whimper.

His voice—*that voice*—drips over my skin like honey laced with venom. It touches every nerve in my body, lighting them up one by one until I'm shaking from a need I can't even understand.

The shadows slither between my thighs, soft and slow. Teasing. Torturous. A breath away from my clit, brushing so close I could cry.

I arch my back, body strung tight as a live wire. "*Please.*"

I don't know what I'm begging for. I just need—*something.*

"Please, what?" he asks, smooth and cruel. "Clarify. I'm not in the mood for vague little tantrums."

"Touch me," I blurt. No filter. Just raw, aching need.

He tilts his head. Smiles. There's a scar across his collarbone now—something new, jagged and cruel. It makes him *real* in a way that only makes everything worse.

"Touch you where, Little Disaster?" he purrs, each word dragging across my skin like a velvet whip.

"Anywhere," I breathe. "Just... *touch me.*"

"You," he says, stepping closer, "will forever be the only woman I get on my knees for." He crosses his arms, leans lazily against a tree like this whole conversation bores him. "Yet you can't even offer me the same decency. Being the *only* male between your legs."

"I *promise!*" I shout, breathless, broken.

"Promise *what?*" he asks, tilting his head again. His eyes are darker now. Hungrier.

I tremble. "I promise it'll be you. Only you. I swear."

This is a dream. Just a dream. Maybe I'm finally cracking and my subconscious is giving me a monogamous monster lover to keep me from combusting.

"*Liar.*"

The word leaves his mouth like a blade. He turns from me like I'm not even worth his time.

"Please!" My voice breaks. "I'm *begging you!* I'll do anything—just fucking *touch* me! *Please!*"

I've never sounded more pathetic in my life. I've also never cared less.

He stops mid-step. Looks over his shoulder with eyes like cold fire.

"You want to be touched?" he says. "*Prove it.* If you can't uphold your promise this time..." He pauses. "You won't like what I do *next* time."

I nod so fast I'm dizzy. "I will. I swear. Just—*please*—I can't take this anymore."

The forest holds its breath.

And then the shadows *devour* me.

They crawl over my body, thick and slick and sentient. Into every crevice. Every *hole*. I don't even fight it—I *welcome* it. My body arches, limbs trembling, a scream torn from my throat as the pleasure hits me like a goddamn freight train.

I'm floating. Falling. Consumed.

And somewhere in the haze of euphoria and shame, I hear him again.

Low. Smug. Unforgiving.

"Sweet dreams, Little Disaster."

CHAPTER NINE

Nyxian

LOVE IS A BITCH - TWO FEET

I could barely fucking control myself.

The second her lips parted to beg—*beg*—I knew I had to get out of there.

My body was seconds away from betraying every principle I've ever forced myself to live by. So I did what I do best. I scared her. I let the shadows snap and hiss and chase. I wrapped them around her and taunted her with what she wanted. With what I wanted.

Because as much as I want to ruin her—I'm not a fucking monster.

I needed her consent. Real consent. I'm not some rabid, unhinged brute.

I lean back in the rickety hospital chair, rubbing my boney chin while the old man in the bed stares at me. Blankly. Quietly. He's heard every word.

"Well," I grunt, "I'm going to help you cross over. For fuck's sake. Just needed to talk to someone first. About my *little disaster.*"

I glance sideways at him. He doesn't blink. Just breathes slow, ragged breaths.

"I listen to you mortals whine and cry about your life's biggest mistakes. The 'I wish I had called her back' and the 'I should've said I love you.' I've heard it all. But I don't have anyone to talk to." I snort. "You should consider yourself lucky. You get a goddamn therapist before death. I get shadows and silence."

The old man rasps a laugh, dry like autumn leaves. "Give her time," he says, voice thin but sure.

"Time?" I sneer. "How much fucking time? Am I supposed to just watch her ruin herself? Watch her spiral into a petri dish of sexual diseases and shitty decisions? What if she gets pregnant by some mortal asshole with a crooked jaw and a vape pen?"

He wheezes a chuckle. "I got my wife to say yes by doing the little things. Took her dancing. Gave her flowers when she was down. We used to sing in the kitchen. She liked old classic country. I can't carry a tune worth shit, but she liked it."

I stare at him.

He hasn't lived as long as I have—not even close. But the bastard has me beat when it comes to mortal women. I've only known them as souls to be judged. Lives to be weighed. Never as beings to be *loved*.

I sigh. Long. Heavy. "You ready, old man?"

He smiles, soft and distant. "Doesn't seem like my granddaughter's gonna make it. Why keep holding on?"

He closes his eyes. "Can I ask you something, though? Something real?"

I glance up at the ceiling like the answer might be carved into the goddamn tiles. "Go for it, Grandpa."

"Does it hurt?" he asks. "When you take me? Will it... hurt?"

He chuckles after the question, like he already knows how ridiculous it sounds.

"No," I murmur, shaking my head. "No pain. Think of it like falling asleep. A long sleep. When you wake up, you're younger. Stronger. Everything that hurts now—gone."

I look at him and allow myself the smallest smile. "Your pain will go away."

His chest rises and falls with one last sigh. "Then I'm ready." A beat of silence, then—"What was your name again?"

The question hits harder than it should.

Startled, I stare at him. Long and quiet.

He doesn't flinch under the weight of it. Just waits.

"My name is Nyxian," I finally say.

He hums, content. "Okay, Nyxian. I'm gonna call you Nyx. That okay?"

I blink. "Yeah. That's okay."

"I'm ready now, Nyx. Can't carry this pain anymore."

My fingers twitch, reaching for the shadows to release his soul, but something stops me.

There's a tightness in my chest I can't explain.

"I can ease some of the pain," I offer, voice quieter. "You sure you don't want to wait a little longer?"

Why the fuck am I offering comfort?

This isn't in my job description.

But he reminds me of someone.

Of *me*.

"Nadia must be busy," he mumbles. "She's a busy girl, that one. Says she'll call me back, but she never does. Always busy. But I wish she would've called me back... just once."

That name.

That fucking name.

A coincidence?

I pull up his profile with a flick of my fingers, like a small screen above his head. And when the name appears on his family tree—my eyes narrow.

Nadia.

His granddaughter is *Nadia.*

Fate, you petty little bitch.

Of *course* it's her.

Of *course* she's tangled in this too.

"You ever wonder if fate just likes to play with us?" I laugh bitterly. "Why would you keep trying if she didn't show she cared?" I ask, genuinely trying to understand.

The old man smiles, tired but full of something I don't quite recognize—*hope*, maybe? Or desperation dressed up like it.

"Because I was hoping," he says, voice cracking like old wood, "that maybe one day, I'd get to hear her say she loved her pawpaw just one more time. Just once more. Just because we're forgotten... doesn't mean we stop trying to feel loved by the people we care about."

The words gut me in a way I don't expect.

They tear right through all the shields I've spent centuries forging.

Because isn't that what I'm doing with *her*?

I reach out, almost without thinking, and grip his frail hand.

It's warm. Real. Mortal.

Everything I'm not.

And still, in that moment, I hold on like it might tether me to something human.

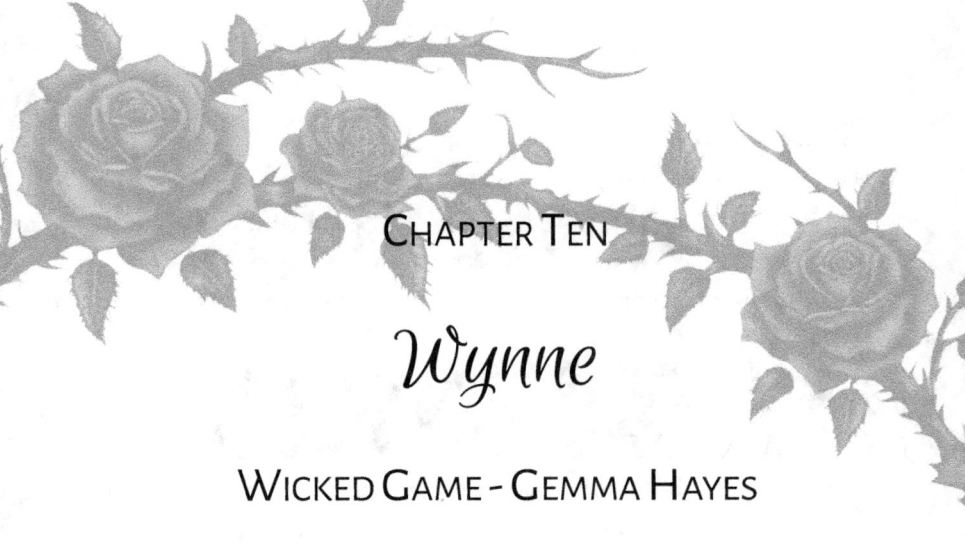

CHAPTER TEN

Wynne

WICKED GAME - GEMMA HAYES

I can't even concentrate on work. I'm a damn mess—half of my words come out jumbled, and I stutter while trying to help customers. It's like my brain short-circuited and just... stopped working. But for now, thank God, the ache between my legs has finally chilled out.

But that dream... That *dream*. It was *too* real, and yet not real enough to be considered an actual memory. I've got bruises around my wrists and ankles, and my room's a disaster. Ryan's belt is still under my bed, but his body? Gone. *Poof.* Vanished like he was never there. I don't even know how to process that.

I log out of my computer, just staring at the screen for a few moments before crawling back into bed, face first into the pillow. Maybe Ryan bored me to sleep? He sure as hell didn't seem the type, but stranger things have happened in my life.

I grab my phone and call him, hoping it's all some sick joke. No answer. His phone's disconnected. I go through my messages and the texts between Ryan and me are gone. *Gone.* Like I imagined every single moment of him.

What. The. Actual. Fuck. Is. Going. On?

I send Nadia a quick text:

> Have you ever had a super real wet dream?

It takes a few seconds for it to be marked as "read," and then the bubbles pop up:

> Girl, yes. Rub one out or call someone to do it for you lol.

I drop the phone beside me, a frustrated sigh escaping my lips as that damn ache starts to creep its way back. For fuck's sake, I need to get a subscription to Sex Addicts Anonymous or something. I roll over, grabbing the phone again and scrolling through my contacts. **Stephen.**

I stare at the screen. What the hell do I even say to him? I'm about as eloquent as a drunk raccoon right now.

> Hey, what's up?

That's all I've got. I drop the phone again, turning to my side.

My mind is still spinning—trying to process the mess with Dylan... or was it Darin? Who the fuck even knows at this point? And then Ryan. Is any of this real? Is it some sort of post-crash trauma? A state of limbo? I can't keep up. This shit doesn't happen to people. *Not to me.*

My phone vibrates, dragging me back to reality. I snatch it up, eyes scanning Stephen's reply:

> Hey girly. Haven't heard from you in a while. Sorry about your loss. How are you holding up?

He's always been so fucking sweet. *Damn it.*

> I'm okay. I guess. I need to get out of the house. You up for an adventure?

I type out, hitting send before I can talk myself out of it.

He replies almost instantly:

I grin at the screen, remembering our first date—years ago now. We went bowling, and then... well, let's just say he didn't exactly stick to *just* knocking the pins out in bowling. The memory makes me tingle. Damn it. Just thinking about it makes me wet.

Yea. Pick me up?

I reply, knowing full well this is going to be one of those nights.

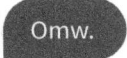

His response is quick, and I feel that little thrill of anticipation bubble up in my chest.

I can't even lie to myself. I'm actually excited. I jump out of bed, rummaging through my closet. I need something easy, but not too easy. I don't want to look like I'm trying too hard, but hell, I don't want to look like a *slob* either. I just want... to be touched. I need to be touched.

I find a pair of shorts that are just long enough to cover my ass, but loose enough for some fingers to weasel their way through... paired with a pink tank top and a small sweater coat. I look in the mirror, throwing on some lip gloss, smacking my lips together like a model in a commercial. I start playing with my hair, trying to decide if I should rock it up or leave it down.

After a few moments of indecision, I think I'm going with an updo. Gotta show off the neck, right? I read something online that said men were *really* attracted to the pheromones women give off from their necks, so hey—*research*, people! Don't let me down now!

I hear a light honk outside, snapping me out of my thoughts. I peek out the window, spotting Stephen's beat-up Chevy truck parked out front. Don't ask me any more questions about it. All I know is there's a huge "Chevy" emblem on the back, and it's covered in dents and rust like it's been through a war. Oh, and it's fucking loud—like, I can hear it from *miles* away. The sound alone is enough to make you think a beast is coming down the street.

I grab my purse, take one last glance at myself in the mirror, and head out the door.

As I step outside, I notice Stephen leaning against the driver's side of his truck, looking all casual, like he's ready for a fun time. His faded blue jeans and worn-out sneakers are about as polished as his truck, but hey, it works for him.

I close the door behind me with a soft click, and the sound of his truck's engine rattles through the air as he waves. "Hey, you look good, girl!" he calls out, flashing me a grin.

"Of course I do. You're lucky to be in my presence," I tease, strutting towards him with my best *"I'm totally not a mess"* vibe.

"Lucky indeed," he mutters, opening the door for me. I climb in, and the instant I'm settled, the truck lurches to life, roaring louder than I expected.

Stephen pulls away from the curb, the truck vibrating beneath me. The ride is bumpy as hell, but it feels oddly comforting in its own way. I glance at him, wondering if he's noticing how my leg keeps bouncing nervously. I'm trying to shake off the dream, trying to focus on the present, but all I can think about is how badly I need to feel something *real* right now.

CHAPTER ELEVEN

Nyxian

YOU WANT A BATTLE? (HERE'S A WAR) - BULLET FOR MY VALENTINE

Does she not learn? I thought I'd given her enough of a reminder that she should just stay the hell away from mortal men. I wish I had eyes to roll—though I can't quite manage it in this form. Still, it doesn't matter. I'll make her regret this if she doesn't stop *testing* me.

She's too fucking stupid to get it. She probably thinks it was just a dream. Dumb bitch. But I'm no dream man. I'm real, and I'll be her fucking *end* if she keeps pushing me.

I watch her roll the ball down the lane, knocking a couple of pins over, and it makes her excited enough to jump into this wannabe Slim Shady's arms. Fucking pathetic.

I move out of sight, avoiding the mortals as I shift into my own mortal form. The transition always leaves me with that pins-and-needles feeling in my limbs, but I don't have time to focus on it. I peek around the corner, seeing them leaning in for a kiss.

Fuck!

Any other mortal woman might have taken the hint. But this dumb bitch? She's surpassed idiocy at this point. I can practically hear her brain scrambling for answers.

I step out from the shadows, my presence enough to make them both freeze. "Got room for one more? Or maybe we make it a challenge—me versus you, and the winner takes the girl home?"

The guy pulls back from her like I've interrupted a fucking fairytale. He looks like a goddamn Ken doll smashed with Eminem—too well-groomed, too clean, and—what the fuck—those piercing blue eyes? *Disgusting*. But is this what she is attracted to?

"Not a chance, bro," he says with that smug, shit-eating grin.

I laugh. It's dark, low, and full of contempt. "Name's Nyxian. But you can call me Nyx." I extend my hand, though I'm not really trying to make a friend. My eyes flicker over to Wynne. She's realizing now, isn't she? The nightmare she thought was a dream is real.

"I'm Stephen," the guy says, shaking my hand like this is just another casual interaction. *Idiot.*

Wynne's eyes snap to me. She asks, "Don't I know you?"

I give her a smile—dark, devious, and full of everything she doesn't want to see. I don't answer her. I don't need to.

Her eyes dart to Stephen, and he notices, looking at her like she's some sort of riddle. He tries to meet her gaze but falters when she locks onto me. I just smirk back, savoring her discomfort.

She's about to get a full fucking dose of reality.

I step closer, making sure my voice is low enough for only her to hear. "Want a..." I pause, dragging the moment out, watching the anticipation build. "Hotdog, Wynne?"

"The fuck?" The look of confusion on Stephen's face is priceless. "How do you know her name?" he asks, eyes narrowing, sensing something off.

"She's my wife," I say casually, shrugging like it's no big deal. Like this is my fucking life.

Stephen blinks at me, completely thrown off. I walk toward the concession stand, where I order a few things with the precision of a male who knows exactly what he's doing— or pretending to know. Two hotdogs, a burger, a small root beer, and two extra-large root beers. Oh, and I make sure to throw in a fully loaded nacho, because why not make this night last?

I head back to them, carrying the tray of food, feeling like I'm walking into a fucking battlefield. Stephen's face is a mix of confusion and fury, and I almost want to laugh. He might fucking implode. I hand him the small root beer, toss Wynne the large one, and set down the burger in front of her—because I don't trust him to get any ideas watching *her* eat the hotdog. She's not for him. She's mine, whether she likes it or not.

Then, I hand him the two hotdogs. Let's see how he eats them. I feel like you can tell a lot about a man by how he eats a hotdog. Does he bite in one go? Does he chew slowly, savoring the taste? Does he deep throat the fuck out of it like the little man fairy he looks?

I sit down next to Wynne with my own food, keeping my eyes locked on Stephen as I smile. The night's just getting started.

"So... *married?*" Stephen asks, his voice full of confusion.

"No." Wynne responds immediately, but I can't help myself.

"Kind of," I say with a smirk, watching Stephen's brow furrow in utter confusion.

He stares between us, trying to piece it together.

"Remember that wreck, my little Disaster?" I throw her a glance, feeling the undeniable pulse of desire coming from her. It makes me smile, just a little. "I fell in love, saving her life. And I try to let her have some fun here and there, but—" I glance up and down Stephen's body with a disdainful sneer. "It seems she's having a *hard time* enjoying herself."

I stand, all my attention now fully on her. "Means it's time for me to come home, right Wynne?"

She stares at me, frozen. She doesn't get it yet, but she will.

Stephen's hand shoots out to grab my arm. "If you're married, where's the ring?" he asks, his voice shaky.

For fuck's sake. I snap my fingers, a sharp crack that makes everyone jump. "She left it in the bathroom, after her little failed attempt to wash me out of her tight little pretty pink pussy." My grin widens as I turn to Wynne, and I watch her blush, the color creeping up her neck.

Stephen's face turns a bizarre shade of red... nearly 50 shades of confusion. His mind struggling to comprehend. It just swirls in his eyes—flabbergasted, unsure, perplexed, and fucking stupefied. *Perfect*. I *thrive* in this *chaos*.

I turn back to Wynne with a look she doesn't yet understand, a silent warning that should've sunk in by now.

Stephen grabs his head, and his eyes are starting to bulge out. Blood begins to trickle from the corners of his eyes, his face twisting in pain.

Screams erupt in the air, filling the space between us, but I just watch.

"Someone call 911!" I yell out, the chaos only fueling the dark satisfaction I'm enjoying. I don't even need to look at the crowd as I grab Wynne's hand and pull her closer.

Time for her punishment. Time for her to finally learn her lesson.

CHAPTER TWELVE

Wynne

DARK SIDE - BISHOP BRIGGS

This fucking stranger—*Nyx*—drags me through the emergency exit of the bowling alley like he's the villain in a romance novel who skipped all the red flags and went straight to the *"get in, loser"* phase. A crowd swarms around Stephen, blocking him from view. I try to look back—because yes, I do care about what is happening to him—but there are too many damn people. I can't even see his discount Air Forces.

Nyx's grip is iron-tight on my wrist. There's zero chance he's letting go. Then he does something absolutely insane—he *hugs* me. Like, body-to-body, heat-to-heat, and before I can process that whiplash, he *kisses* me. And not a *"hey, we're friends now"* kind of kiss—no, this is the kind of kiss that rewrites your personality and probably fries a brain cell or two.

Next thing I know, we're in my room.

"What the hell?" I look around, completely disoriented. "How did we get here?"

"*Magic.*" He does spirit fingers in my face like he's a deranged fairy godfather.

I just blink at him.

"I thought we discussed this already," he mutters, dropping into my bedroom chair like he owns it—manspreading like a goddamn villain in an expensive cologne commercial. My heart skips. My stomach flips. I think my ovaries did a cartwheel, perhaps.

Okay, Wynne. Time to book a therapy appointment. Like, yesterday.

He just sits there, staring. Unbothered. Like he's got *nothing but time* to haunt me and my ovaries into oblivion.

"You're taking this a lot better than I thought you would," he says, casually propping his chin in his hand, those long, sharp fingers looking like they've done unspeakable things... and maybe will do unspeakable things to me.

"Yeah, well. You hit the jackpot, dude. I'm all kinds of messed up." I collapse onto the bed with a sigh. "Honestly, if a masked burglar broke into my house, he'd leave either really satisfied or deeply traumatized."

Nothing. Not a smile. Not a single damn laugh. Just... *Nyxian*, staring at me like I'm the entertainment and he already knows the plot twist.

"I have work in the morning," I mumble, toeing off my shoes.

"No, you don't." He says it like it's a universal truth.

"Uh. Yeah. I do." I give him a look.

He just rolls his eyes, then strolls over to my closet like *he* pays the rent. "I put your resignation in."

"I'm sorry... what?"

"You don't have to work anymore," he says, not even glancing at me while he starts pulling out things from a drawer that I absolutely forgot existed. "Your sole job now is to be at my beck and call."

"Excuse me?"

"You heard me, my Little Disaster. You exist now to please me. Emotionally, physically, spiritually—hell, maybe metaphysically, too."

He emerges with a strap in one hand, a few toys in the other, and a look that says *you're about to be wrecked emotionally and then ruined spiritually*. My inner chaos gremlin is shrieking. Very fucking loudly.

I stand up just to pretend like I have any control over this situation. "We don't even get to play 20 Questions first? Maybe an awkward icebreaker or two? You know, to delay the weird kinky power play that's obviously about to happen?"

He tilts his head, those obsidian eyes flashing with something way too dangerous. "Really? You want to play a game?" He sits at the edge of the bed, laying everything he brought out like some kind of unholy buffet.

He runs his fingers along each item, slow and deliberate, like he's checking the sharpness of knives. It's weirdly hot. *Help!*

"I don't even know you and you're just—planning to... you know..." I gesture vaguely at the pile of things that scream *you're not walking straight tomorrow*.

"What do you want to know?" His voice is syrupy dark, smooth with an edge. Then he smiles, and I swear those canines weren't that sharp earlier.

"Where were you born?"

"The Underworld."

I laugh. "No, for real."

"For real." He flips a switch on a toy, the soft buzz slicing through the tension like a blade. "My turn now."

I blink. "Excuse me?"

"How about this?" He leans in slightly. "Every time you manage *not* to orgasm, you earn a question or a random fact about me. A piece of the puzzle."

He picks up a restraint, his fingers caressing the leather like it's something precious.

I stare at him, momentarily speechless. I have to *resist* climaxing to get answers? What kind of evil reverse psychology mind game is this?

Easy. He's a stranger. I can totally keep it together.

Right?

Then why am I already on edge? Why is my body reacting to the sound of his voice like it's a goddamn playlist of all my weaknesses?

Focus, Wynne. Pull it together, you chaotic little goblin.

Nyx installs the restraints like he's done it a thousand times. His outfit? All black. His vibe? Chaos and control in perfect harmony.

He is darkness personified—and I'm about to find out what happens when the dark doesn't just touch you...

...but you fucking want it to.

"Weren't you ever taught not to stare?" Nyxian growls.

He doesn't even glance at me while slipping the end of a restraint through the loop, anchoring it to the bedpost like it's a totally normal Tuesday activity. Meanwhile, I'm standing here wondering how the hell I went from bowling alley chaos to bedroom bondage in the span of two kisses and a teleportation spell.

Words. Yes, those. Where are they again?

"Why did you choose me?" I manage, voice hoarse, barely a whisper.

He looks over his shoulder, gaze impassive. "I was bored."

Asshole. The word smacks into my brain like a brick, but before I can launch it at him with appropriate spice, he continues.

"I've lived my life for the role given to me. Immortality means nothing if you don't get to live." He straightens, still not looking at me. "I've been underestimated my entire existence. Then fate shoved your chaos into my path like a cosmic dare." He finally turns to face me, eyes unreadable. "You've been underestimated too. Overlooked. Unappreciated."

He tosses a vibrator onto the bed like he's throwing down a gauntlet. My brain short-circuits at the casual absurdity of it all.

The air between us thickens.

"No more questions now," he says, voice low. "Get undressed."

"Fucking excuse me?" The words launch themselves from my mouth before I can stop them.

"I'm not going to repeat myself, Little Disaster." His arms cross. "Undress. Or I'll show you what happens when you test me."

Tempting. So very tempting to see what he means by that—but something primal flickers deep inside, telling me that he isn't bluffing. This man is all follow-through and feral promises.

So, I toe off my shoes. I strip my shirt over my head, hesitating as I reach for the clasp of my bra.

That's when I feel him.

Warmth. Body heat, pressure, the quiet crackle of static between us. His hands find my waist, slow and sure. I should pull away. I should scream, throw a punch, remind him that I'm nobody's to command.

But I don't.

Because when he's this close, something inside me stills.

It's not peace. It's something sharper—like the moment before lightning touches ground.

His breath is hot against my skin as he leans in, unclasping my bra with practiced ease. I hate that my skin responds. Goosebumps ripple down my arms, my spine. My body betrays me. *Again.*

He lingers—breath against my neck, a soft graze of lips up to my ear. "I can smell how badly you want to be *touched*."

I let out a strangled sound, half a moan, half a "what the hell is wrong with me" gasp, when he grabs a handful of my hair and pulls just enough to tilt my face toward his.

His eyes are fire and void. "You are *mine*, Wynne."

The words sink into my chest like brands.

My panties are gone. I didn't even feel him slide them down. I should care more about that, right?

"I'm not going to fuck you *today*." His voice is velvet over steel. "You haven't earned that, Little Inferno. But when I do?" He pauses, brushing fingers along my hip. "You won't be able to think of anyone else ever again."

My heart is pounding so loud I'm sure he can hear it.

He steps back, gestures to the bed. "Lie down."

And I do.

No hesitation. No sass.

That terrifies me more than anything else.

Because this is real. Not a book. Not a fantasy. Not some spicy chapter I dog-eared at 2 a.m. with my favorite vibrator.

And yet—I'm not screaming. I'm not fighting. I'm lying down on the bed, mad that he *isn't* going to fuck me.

What the actual hell is wrong with me?

I can see the bulge in his pants.

Jesus.

It's not subtle. It's *impossible* to ignore. The kind of outline that makes your mouth go dry and your brain go fuzzy. He looks *huge*. Like *ruin-me-from-the-inside-out* huge. Like I'll walk different for a week, huge. He looks human. But that bulge? That thing is not.

Something about it whispers in the back of my head that once he has me—really has me—I won't ever come back the same. And maybe I don't want to.

I swallow hard, forcing my eyes away from it and up to his face. He smirks like he knows exactly what I'm staring at. Like he's *used* to being stared at. Like he's used to being worshipped, feared, maybe even fucking *desired*.

I hate that he's winning right now. This is a game now.

I didn't agree to the rules, but I'm still playing. I'm a sore loser, always have been. I can't stand the idea of him getting under my skin without me clawing my way under his in return.

So I already know what I'm going to ask him first.

I'm going to flip this power. Crack his cool. Peel the mask off the monster and make him *feel* something.

And maybe—just maybe—I'll win.

Even if it kills me.

CHAPTER THIRTEEN

Nyxian

GOD'S GUNNA CUT YOU DOWN - MARILYN MANSON

I can see it in her eyes—the defiance, the spark. She's goading me, and I let her.

No, worse—*I crave it.*

She smiles like she's already won, but she doesn't know the war she's starting. I didn't expect this to feel like torture... *for me.* I'm supposed to be in control, yet I can already feel the tension clawing through me, heat sinking into my spine like venom.

If I so much as shift in my stance, she'll see it.

See the weakness.

See that *she* has this effect on me.

And I'll be damned before I give her that satisfaction.

I fasten the restraints at her wrists and ankles—slowly, deliberately, watching the way her breath catches with each one. She lays on the bed like temptation personified, all soft curves and fire-lit defiance. Her hair fans around her head like a wildfire caught mid-bloom, and those ridiculous blue eyes—damn them—are locked onto mine with something that shouldn't make me pause.

But it does.

I step back. Arms crossed.

She's laid out in front of me, bound and beautiful, and I have never wanted to ruin someone so perfectly in my life. Not like this. She's spread wide for me, I can see the pink between her legs and I have to resist the urge to taste her.

A collection of implements sits on the nightstand—gifts from realms she'll never walk freely. Tools of pleasure, of pain, of power. I reach for the wand. It looks innocuous in my grip, like a child's toy. Innocent. Powerless.

It's not.

I am not.

She watches me, eyes wide with something between challenge and surrender. It isn't fear. It's curiosity. Trust, maybe, hidden beneath every smart-mouthed jab she's thrown at me since the moment we met.

That alone is more intimate than anything I've done to her.

Wynne will be my mate even if she doesn't accept it right away. I have to *show* her how dedicated I am to her.

I take my time looking at her—*really* looking. Every freckle scattered over her skin like stardust. They say they're the kisses of Guardian Angels. If that's true, then I want that bastard angel dead for daring to touch her.

Especially when he was the one who was supposed to fucking protect her.

I will find that fucker and behead him for touching his lips to her body without her consent. What I am doing is different. My little slut *wants* this. She is aware of my existence. She *wants* me to fuck her.

My perfect Little Disaster.

I know what she's been through. What was done to her. I've read the files. Dug up the memories the moment I sensed she wasn't just another beautiful mortal playing pretend.

There's more to her than she likes to let on. I have been doing research on her — trying to figure out if I made a mistake, but no. Fate put her in my path because she is *reckless*, self-destructive— but not at her own free will.

She has been molested by her uncle since she was three. A man I have already wiped from this planet— this fucking realm. Ruptured his soul and fed it to the Keres as a fucking snack so he *can't* come back for another life cycle. Eric didn't stand a chance. I let him *beg* for mercy like Wynne *begged* for him to stop.

Her uncle is ash now. I made sure of it. There was no mercy. Not a whisper of it. I watched him bleed into the soil of the realm he'll never crawl back from.

He will not hurt her again.

I rest my hand on her hip, tracing down the line of her thigh, watching how she reacts—how she breathes differently when I get close. My fingers follow a silent trail guiding me to her pussy. Her skin trembles beneath my touch. Not from fear. Not from pain.

From *want*.

I lean close. My voice is low. Dark.

"Tell me you want me."

Wynne wishes to cum, and I will make her do *just* that despite the little game we have going on right now between us. This is *her* choice. I won't prey on her like every mortal and immortal man or male have. Those disgusting "men" and her pig of a Guardian Angel. If I didn't come when I did, she would have—no doubt— been impregnated by him only to birth a sleeping baby of this world, and a Guardian Angel for mine.

She blinks up at me, lips parted, voice quiet but clear.

"I want you."

Gods help me.

The flicker of warmth in my chest makes me furious.

"*Beg*," I growl. "Beg me, Wynne."

Her lips curl into a smirk, but her eyes darken. "Please, Nyx. Please... I need to feel your hands on me."

She's about to erupt right here, right now. She's so wet... for *me*. The sound of my name in her mouth. Soft. Desperate.

I hate it.

I love it.

She doesn't know what she's doing to me.

No—maybe she *does*.

And she's winning.

She's close.

Too close.

She trembles beneath me, breath shallow, body straining at the restraints like she's seconds from detonation. Her skin shines with heat and want—and *gods*, she's soaked for *me*. All for me.

I thumb the wand to life, setting the pattern to something erratic. Rhythmic, teasing. Like a heartbeat with no loyalty to hers. She's about to learn something she's never been taught—*discipline*. And if she wants to win, she'll have to earn it.

Hovering the tool just above where she craves it most, I watch her push against her restraints—desperate, ready to take whatever I give her.

"Please, Nyx," she breathes, her voice barely there—dreamlike, dizzy.

I give in.

Just a taste.

I press the tool to her, and her reaction is instant. Her moan punches straight through me like a weapon, echoing in my head, ricocheting down my spine. Her back arches, eyes fluttering closed, then rolling back as if her body can't handle the sensation. The wand pulses against her, then stills, then pulses again—cruel and inconsistent. But she doesn't complain.

She *thanks* me with every gasp.

Every sigh.

Every twitch.

She's sweat-slicked now, and I watch a bead roll down the side of her face before I pull the wand away.

She groans, frustration seeping from every pore.

I smirk. "Want a fact or a question?"

She doesn't answer right away. Her chest rises and falls like she's running from something, even though she's chained down and begging for more.

Then, quietly, "What are you?"

Her voice is hoarse. Raw.

I step toward the head of the bed and cradle her jaw in my palm. Tilting her chin until she meets my eyes. She blinks herself back into the moment. She's dazed, undone, but holding on.

Good.

She still has fight in her.

"I'm a Grim Reaper," I say, my voice low and bitter.

She doesn't ask the follow-up. Doesn't press. Just *sees* me. And I don't like the way her gaze cracks something inside me open.

Her pain lives in those blue eyes. Hidden. Buried beneath every sarcastic remark and fiery comeback. She's a fortress made of broken glass, trying to pretend she isn't shattered.

And *damn it all,* I want to keep her from splintering further.

I hate that feeling.

I hate *her* for making me feel it.

I release a long breath and step back. "A Grim Reaper isn't like your average soul-sweeper. I'm one of the old ones. Strong enough to wield a tool."

"A tool?" she repeats, her voice laced with curiosity.

I show her—not by words, but by action.

A flick of my fingers, and the room dips in shadow. A ribbon of darkness rises from the corner, slithering toward her skin like it knows her.

Because it does.

Because it's *a part of me.*

I let it brush against her—just enough to make her gasp and press herself into the mattress. Her moan this time is different. Not from pleasure alone. It's from awe. From connection.

I pull the shadow back and release her face gently.

My fingers twitch toward the pile of toys again.

I'm not done with her. Not until she's unraveling in my name, not until she forgets every mortal man who came before me, not until she begs me like I'm the only one who's ever made her feel anything real.

Because I am.

And she'll know it.

She'll scream it.

I reach for one of the toys—one I remember seeing tucked away in her digital wish list. A silicone piece, rainbow-colored and laced with silver flecks like stardust frozen mid-spark. Cute. Fitting. Deceptively *innocent.*

It hums to life in my hand, mechanical and relentless, thrusting rhythmically while vibrating deep. I glance up.

Wynne's eyes widen for a moment—then she throws her head back against the pillows, red hair splayed like wildfire.

I step closer, slipping my hand between her thighs. She's trembling. I spread her gently, watching every twitch of anticipation ripple through her. With care, I guide the toy to her and ease it in. Her hips buck at the first press of movement. She lets out a moan that tightens something sharp and volatile inside me.

I grit my teeth.

My control frays.

But I'm *not* finished.

I lower myself between her legs, letting my breath graze her before my mouth follows. I give her one slow, deliberate stroke of my tongue across the bundle of nerves she's keeping hostage beneath that moan. Her body jolts like a live wire.

"Oh, *fuck,*" she cries, voice cracking around the edges of pleasure.

I swallow a growl. My smile curves against her skin as I let my teeth graze her thigh, marking her without breaking the surface. I glance up—and our eyes lock.

Something primal ignites.

The sight of her unraveled, bare and writhing because of *me,* is more than just satisfying—it's addictive. A fire roars in my blood. A dangerous, all-consuming instinct to take her right here, *right now,* no barriers, no *limits.* I want to feel every inch of her pussy pulsing around me while she calls out my name like a fucking prayer.

I have this feral urge to pull the dildo out and insert myself, but *I* need to be patient.

I can't.

Not yet.

I'm not done showing her she belongs to me in more ways than one.

I pull back slowly, tongue flicking over my bottom lip as I rise to my full height.

She whimpers—needy, raw, absolutely ruined—and I've barely even started.

Chapter Fourteen

Wynne

Devil's Backbone - The Civil Wars

I'm trying not to vibrate off the bed. My body's shaking, and I'm clenching every muscle I have to teach myself how to not moan like I'm auditioning for a damn romance audiobook.

Think of anything but Nyxian. Dead bodies. Something gross. Darryl's corpse. Or was it Dixon? David? Doesn't matter—whoever he was, thanks for your service to my sanity.

I suck in a breath, trying to focus. I *will* win this game. I already know what my last question will be—something ridiculous, something totally off-the-wall that will throw him off just enough to give me an edge. But right now? I'm hanging on by a thread.

My hips jerk against the toy with a mind of their own, and all that escapes me is a mess of grunts, gasps, and some very unladylike whimpers. We're locked in a stare-off, like two predators. Only I'm definitely the one tied to the bed... so yeah. Predatory disadvantage.

Then, without warning, he pulls the toy from my body, turns it off, and—*licks* it. My jaw drops.

"I've never tasted something so addicting," Nyxian says, his voice pure sin.

"Well," I pant, arching up off the bed like a woman possessed, "how about you stop teasing and go face-deep, Reaper."

His smile is all teeth, dark and wicked. He places the toy down beside what suspiciously looks like a wand from a certain famous wizarding franchise. "Fact or question?"

"Hit me with a random fact."

He stands, eyeing his carefully curated collection of torture—I mean, plea-sure—devices. He picks up something that looks like a fancy sea shell with tech built into it. A sucker. Fabulous. My impending god damned doom.

And are his nails painted black? Of course they are.

"As a Reaper, I'm not allowed to sleep," he says casually, like he's talking about skipping lunch, not violating all laws of mortal sanity.

I blink. "I'm sorry... what?"

"I was a late bloomer. Reaper training starts at age three. I didn't start until seven." He strolls up to the head of the bed, casual as ever, and leans against the wall like this isn't the most bonkers thing I've ever heard.

"Okay, I know I'm not supposed to ask questions during your little game, but—Nyxian. What?"

He nods once, solemn. "In the Underworld, we're created with intent. Some are bred to be soldiers, others Reapers, some for other services. Some don't survive long enough to become anything at all. I was meant to be a soldier, but they made me a Reaper instead. So I trained for both."

He perches on my nightstand like this is coffee shop conversation and not the kind of thing that makes my head spin.

"So... why start that young?" I ask, still trying to absorb this.

"So it becomes instinct. We don't remember anything else. We become what they need us to be."

I stare at him. He's not showing much emotion—but something flickers behind his eyes, and it isn't indifference.

"Why can't you sleep?" I ask, a bit softer this time.

"One hundred and twenty-one mortals die every minute. One Reaper per death. That's a minimum of 121 active at any given time. There are roughly 7,500 Reapers running at any hour."

"Holy hell..." I whisper. "Are all Reapers... *men*?"

"We aren't bound by mortal gender, but we use it for convenience. Male, female. It doesn't define us. But no, we aren't all males." He rises and circles back to the foot of the bed like a predator pacing.

The restraints dig into my wrists as I tug. Not in pain. In *desperation*. I *will* survive this round. I *will* win.

"When does this end?" I ask, voice rasping.

He smirks. "When you moan my name. And you will."

I laugh—more out of stubborn defiance than amusement. "I think you've met your match, Reaper. I don't lose gracefully. Want to make it interesting?"

His eyes narrow. "Go on."

"If I win, you eat me out, and then screw me like you fucking hate me."

His brows arch in amusement. "Pretty sure using sex as leverage is illegal in the mortal realm."

I give him a devilish grin. "Yeah, well... you're not mortal, are you?"

"Touché." He turns the shell on. It starts to hum in a stop-and-go rhythm. Pulsing. Teasing. The kind of setting that was clearly designed by someone who hated self-control and was interested in morse code for orgasm calling.

I swallow hard.

This man is going to ruin me.

And I'm going to let him.

He lowers it over my clit, positioning the toy right over it. I let out a *scream*, "Fuck!"

It pulls and sucks my clit, my toes curl.

Dead. Body. Dead. Body. Dead. Body.

Then it stops abruptly.

One Mississippi.

Two Mississippi.

Then it starts again. We lock eyes once more, butterflies flutter in my stomach.

"You're doing *so* good, Little Disaster. You are so fucking *wet*. I almost wish you do win so I can feel it around my dick."

He leans down and kisses right below my belly button.

The sucking stops again– but it doesn't give me time to gather my thoughts before it starts again. I can feel how *close* I am being tipped over the edge... the urge to call his name out – but I *have* to win.

I can't let him win this. I've already decided what my last question will be, and I'll make sure it's the perfect one. The key to victory is in my hands.

I'm trying to keep my body from betraying me, my legs trembling with the effort. I think about anything but what's happening—my mind flicks to Dylan... no... Darryl. *Fuck!*

What was his name?

Damon?

Dennis?

Darin!

His name *was Darin!*

It stops again. I let out the breath I was holding and before I could catch my breath again – it starts again. Pulling my clit into the toy, vibrating and sucking it.

I'm *about* to cum!

Fuck! Think, Wynne – *Think!*

I fight the urge to react to the way his touch feels, the pressure, the pulse. I need to hold on. I have to.

We lock eyes, a challenge between us that burns hotter than any fire. His smirk is devilish, knowing exactly what he's doing to me.

He pauses, taking the tool away, and I can't help the frustrated noise that escapes my lips. My body is too far gone, too aware of every tiny shift, every gentle tug.

"Fact or question?" he asks, voice low and teasing.

"I don't want to play this anymore," I mutter, my voice shaky from the overwhelming sensations.

"Tsk... Tsk. You know how to stop this, Little Disaster." Nyx's voice is low and teasing as he walks back up to the head of the bed.

"Well, if I quit, I wouldn't get to brag about 'fucking a Grim Reaper,' now, would I?" I exhale, trying to still the tremors in my body, desperate for some release.

He leans down, his breath warm against my ear. "You won't be able to brag. You won't even be able to leave this bed," he says, his laugh soft but full of menace.

"Why won't you just give in and end this already?" I challenge, my voice barely above a whisper, but my body betrays me, thrumming with need.

"Is this your question?" He doesn't wait for an answer, and I can feel his gaze on me, sharp, intense.

I try to fight it. "Screw you," I snap, but even I can hear the way my voice falters.

"Is it... your... question?" He leans in, his thumb lightly brushing over my nipple, making it hard to think straight.

"Yes!" The word comes out in a breathless whisper, and I hate that I'm giving in so easily.

"Because you haven't earned it yet, Little Disaster." His words are almost a taunt as he pulls back and strolls to the foot of the bed, surveying his collection of toys. But is it torture if I like it? Arrogant bastard.

I grumble, trying to press my thighs together in an attempt to relieve the ache that's building.

He picks up a toy, its sleek design gleaming in the dim light. "I don't get pleasure with anal. Do you?" His voice is casual, but there's an edge to it, a challenge.

I roll my eyes. "Shit dick is not my thing, Nyxian. Does that count as a question for you?"

He smirks, the glint of amusement in his eyes. "Nyx will do. Maybe 'daddy' one day." He winks, a teasing lilt to his voice.

I can't help but smirk back. "I'd love to call you daddy, but that requires you to actually, you know, do something first. I think *'asshole'* works better for now." The words slip out before I can stop them, my own challenge dripping with defiance.

He moves toward me, his body coming over mine in a smooth, controlled motion. I feel his presence, his heat, and I can't ignore the way his body presses against mine—just enough to make me crave more.

"Do you know why I won't give in yet?" His voice is a whisper, but the tension in it is undeniable.

I shake my head, my breath shallow as he grinds against me, barely enough to satisfy the ache but enough to keep me on edge.

"Because you're a promise breaker," he says softly, his lips grazing my neck. "What would your mortals call it? A *cheater*. And Wynne, I don't like to share. You're mine and *only mine*." His words send a thrill through me, though I refuse to let him see how much they affect me.

I tilt my head, my cheek brushing against his. "I promise, if you can prove to me you're worth it, I'll be your good girl, Nyx."

He moans softly, and I can tell I've hit a nerve. "And what happens if you fuck up?" he asks, his voice dark.

I nibble on his ear. "You can use your own discretion."

His hand slips between us, teasing, coaxing, and I can't hold back the moan that escapes me.

"Untie me, Nyx. Please," I beg, my voice a rasp. "So I can wrap myself around you."

His fingers pause, his eyes locking onto mine. "Moan my name," he commands, a dark promise in his gaze.

"No," I say with a sly smile, despite my need. "I won this round. You touched me with something other than a toy. Are you a man of your word, Nyx?"

He chuckles, low and deep, his eyes gleaming with something dangerous. "Very sly. But I suppose you're right."

"Then prove it. Make good on your word." My voice is steady, daring him to follow through.

He slides off of me and settles at the foot of the bed, eyes gleaming with purpose. "I told you before—you're the only woman I'd ever get on my knees for. That includes my past as well."

Then, without hesitation, he lowers his head between my thighs.

The first touch of his mouth steals the breath from my lungs. My head falls back, my body arches, every muscle tightening with the storm of sensation. I can't move—I want to grab him, to guide him, but my wrists are still bound, leaving me helpless under his control.

His tongue moves with deliberate, devastating precision, finding every sensitive spot, teasing and exploring as if memorizing me.

My cries echo in the room when his focus shifts, his lips closing around my most sensitive point, his tongue flicking with a merciless rhythm. I shatter—utterly undone—my body trembling with the force of release.

Nyx doesn't stop.

He shifts, mouth still locked to me, and reaches up to unbuckle the restraints at my ankles. My legs are free and before I even realize it—I am wrapping them instinctively around his shoulders, pulling him closer, deeper. His hands are firm on my hips, holding me in place while his tongue continues its devastating work.

Then he pulls back, breath heavy, face flushed.

His fingers move to the waistband of his pants. I watch—entranced, breathless—as he slides them down, followed by his boxers. When he straightens, he pulls his shirt over his head, and my breath catches.

Scars mar his chest and sides, long and jagged, evidence of battles I've never seen.

"What are those from?" I ask, voice barely more than a whisper.

"Training." His answer is simple, but the weight behind it lingers. He steps forward, releasing my wrists with careful fingers. "Are you sure you're ready for this?"

His eyes—usually full of shadows—now burn with a rare vulnerability. I nod, pulling him into a kiss that's hungry, aching, *desperate*. His mouth meets mine, his tongue slipping in and tasting like smoke and heat.

He shifts, one arm supporting his weight while the other reaches down. I feel him press against me, teasing with gentle, deliberate strokes from his cock.

"If I hurt you," he murmurs, voice rough against my ear, "tell me."

I can't speak. I just shake my head, already overwhelmed.

When he begins to push into me, the stretch is intense—almost too much—but I cling to him, wrapping my legs around his waist, holding him there. He moves slowly, his hips finding a rhythm, his body guiding mine through each inch of pressure.

It's overwhelming. *He's overwhelming.*

But I want *more.*

"Moan. My. Name." His voice is a command, breathless.

I turn my head, cheek brushing against his arm. "Why?"

"Do it."

I surrender. "Nyx," I whisper, then say it louder. "*Nyx!*"

That's all it takes.

Something snaps inside him. His control fractures. His hips slam into mine with a force that knocks the breath from my lungs. He moves faster, harder, a growl vibrating from his chest as he pours himself into every thrust.

I hold on, completely consumed.

I can feel him releasing inside of me, a warm squirt of hot liquid. *Fuck,* that was good.

And when it's over—when the world stills and all that's left is the sound of our breaths tangled together—I know something has changed.

He's claimed me.

And I fucking let him.

CHAPTER FIFTEEN

Wynne

THE WAY I DO - BISHOPP BRIGGS

T his can't be my life.

Did I enjoy it? *Yes.*

Would I do it again? Also yes.

But this has *got* to be a fever dream. No way is there a Grim Reaper—*the* Grim Reaper—sprawled out in my bed like it's just another Tuesday.

No way did I just fuck a Grim Reaper.

I peek out from behind the bathroom door, clutching a towel to my chest like it can protect me from the realization that I've completely lost my mind.

He's just... lying there. *Naked.* Staring at the ceiling like he's contemplating the mysteries of the universe—or maybe just thinking about waffles. I can't tell.

What the hell is he waiting for? What's he thinking about? What does he *want*?

I tiptoe out of the bathroom, still very naked and very cold. Like, *nipples-could-cut-glass* cold. I shiver all the way to my closet and grab the first thing I can find that looks warm enough to thaw my poor soul—a floor-length pink nightgown with a satin finish and a neckline that still manages to say *hello, cleavage.*

Great. Why am I trying to look good for this guy? This asshole? *Ugh.*

I sigh, loud and full of drama, just in time for Nyxian to sneak up on me like a freaking ghost. His hand lands on my shoulder and I *scream* like I'm in a horror movie.

"The *fuck*, Nyx!"

He looks startled but not sorry. "I was just checking on you." He rubs the back of his neck like that'll make it better. "I can feel your emotions in the room. They're... heavy."

I blink at him. Top to bottom. This man is disgustingly gorgeous. Even soft, he's still got that same thick, intimidating length and—

Nope. *Focus, Wynne.*

"I'm fine." I say it flatly, trying to summon even an ounce of chill.

He nods, but I know he's not buying it. He probably knows I'm mentally spiraling about the fact that I just had sex with a stranger who *teleported* me home, tied me up, and gave me a spiritual awakening with his mouth.

Normal things.

He casually walks across the room and sits in the chair in the corner like he owns the place. "How long have you known Nadia?"

My brow furrows. "Nadia? Why?"

"Her grandfather died."

I freeze. "Paw Paw Charles?"

He nods.

"I... I didn't even know he was sick." My chest tightens as I sit on the edge of my bed. "How do *you* know this?"

"I walked him to judgment," he says simply, like it's just another bullet point on his to-do list. "He asked me to wait. He thought she'd come say goodbye."

I go quiet. He's watching me—really watching me—with a stare that's too trained, too focused.

"The thing about mortals," he says, "is they don't respect the people who paved the way for them to screw everything up in the first place."

A sting forms behind my eyes. "I didn't know. I would've been there if I did."

"It wasn't *you* he wanted to see before he passed." His voice is lower now. "It was *her*. His granddaughter."

"I've known Nadia most of my life. Her family's like mine. I should've been there."

"But you weren't. And neither was she. What's done is done." He stands, pulling on his clothes with that same casual ease that makes me want to throw something at his head.

"Where are you going?" I blurt.

Not because I want him to stay. Obviously. Totally *not* that. But who drops emotional bombs and then *leaves*?

"I have work," he says, shrugging on his shirt. "I'll be back later."

"What if I'm not here?" I challenge.

He walks up to me, cups my chin like I'm made of something fragile, and tilts my face to his. "I'll *always* find you."

...Not creepy at all.

Then he disappears. Just *poof*. Gone. Like some sexy, emotionally unavailable shadow daddy with a magical dick game.

I exhale, looking around the room like maybe he'll pop back up and say "just kidding," but nope. No Nyx.

Still holding my breath, I grab my phone and call Nadia. The ringing feels like static in my ear.

Then she answers. "I was *just* about to call you, bitch! Let's go to NOLA!"

"For what?" I ask, blinking.

She scoffs. "Do you *need* a reason to go to NOLA?"

I laugh, but there's a lump in my throat now. When do I tell her about Paw Paw Charles? Does she know already? Is *this* how she's coping?

Before I can say anything, she sings, "I'm outside. Come on!"

I panic, hang up, and start tearing through the room for something to wear. My original clothes are still on the floor from the whole *Nyxian threw me over his shoulder and wrecked my existence* moment, so I throw those on in a rush.

By the time I dart out the door, Nadia's car is waiting— along with two of the scariest guys I have ever seen crammed inside.

I pause at the passenger door, waiting for the dude in the seat to take the hint and *move*. When he doesn't, Nadia slaps him. Hard. He scrambles out, and I slide in like nothing happened.

She grins. I shoot her a look.

Then, with zero explanation, she speeds off like we're late for a heist.

And just like that, my life is officially a dumpster fire in a hurricane. With fucking glitter.

CHAPTER SIXTEEN

Nyxian

JUDGEMENT DAY - STEALTH

F inding Wynne's Guardian Angel wasn't hard. Pathetic little bastard wasn't even hiding.

He's in queue, waiting like a good dog for his next assignment. *Felix.* Fucking *Felix.*

He got the boot the second I made Wynne immortal. That should've been the end of it. No second chances. No new mortal to defile. But the system drags its feet when it comes to accountability. So I did a little digging. And surprise, surprise—he's a predator. With fucking wings.

I spot him at a café near the Veil, stuffing his face, picking his teeth like some local hero with a stomach full of sin. He waves off the waitress with a bloated smirk and waddles out like he owns the place he's squatting in. The Underworld's red light spills onto his greasy skin, casting him in blood.

It suits him.

My stomach twists at the sight. Disgusting. And those wings—those feathered frauds—rest against his bare back like they *deserve* to be there. He's shirtless like he's proud of what he is.

I don't claim this sibling. I won't. Not even a little. Vassago's going to come barking soon, all self-righteous and bleeding-heart, but I don't care. Wynne's worth every ounce of fallout. I'd burn the Underworld to ash if it meant protecting her.

I pick up my pace, closing the distance, and slam my fist into the back of his head. Hard.

Felix stumbles forward, groaning, clutching his skull like he didn't fucking deserve that. When he turns around, I'm already standing there, hands in my pockets, calm as a corpse.

"The fuck, Nyxian?" he spits. His voice grates on me. High-pitched. Slimy. Weak.

I take a slow step forward. "By law, you're supposed to be executed."

His brow furrows. "For what?"

Another step. Shadows curl at my feet, stretching like claws. "For touching a mortal woman you were meant to protect. Guardian Angels aren't permitted to fuck their charges."

He scoffs, full of that false bravado cowards wear when they know they've been caught. "You're talking about that little slut you claimed?"

The shadows snap forward before he can take another breath, yanking his ankles out from under him. He crashes to the ground, and I step over him like garbage.

"How's that working out for you, by the way?" he sneers, trying to crawl to his feet.

I don't answer. He's not owed one.

Instead, I tighten the shadows around his limbs. I let them taste his skin—whipping the skin on his ankles— drawing blood. "You've got two options. I can end you here, in this alley no one will remember... or we can bring this to Azrael and Vassago."

He struggles, but there's no escaping me. He *knows* it.

"Fuck you, Nyxian! You and I both know Vassago won't let the angels fall. He'll protect me. Just like always."

There it is. The coward's gospel. Depend on someone else to clean up your rot.

Fine.

I summon the darkness again, swirling it into a portal. A shortcut through the Veil, straight to Azrael's last known location. Felix screams as the shadows drag him behind me, bones scraping the ground, wings limp.

He made a mistake thinking I cared about the consequences.

He'll learn.

They *all* will.

We appear at the Sandman's home, shadows shifting beneath my feet, Felix dragging behind me like the filth he truly is. Guards line the path to the front door. I nod to the one stationed closest, who eyes Felix with thinly veiled curiosity but doesn't question me.

I knock once. Firm. Loud. Unapologetic.

The door opens a moment later to reveal a woman—mortal, clearly—with wild black curls and huge brown eyes that blink up at me like she's never seen a seven-foot shadow-drenched problem on her porch before.

"Can I help you?" she asks, voice sweet like sugared poison.

"Yes, madam. I was hoping to catch one of my brothers. The matter is... *pressing*." I gesture to Felix still bound and twitching at my feet.

She leans slightly, spots him—and then smiles? "Death boy! You have a rather tall, dark, and mighty fine shadow daddy at the door!"

I cough. Orcus hums with pure glee around the corner within the house.

"Shadow daddy," he muses. "I *am* putting that on a T-shirt."

Azrael rounds the corner in his mortal form, scowling. "Sadie! Use our *real* names when it comes to Underworld business."

He notices me, then Felix, and stops just short of sighing.

"Nyxian," he greets warily, "everything okay?"

"I do like the *'shadow daddy'* term," Orcus adds, echoing just to be an ass. "It feels... accurate. Regal. Kinky."

Ignoring them both, I shove Felix forward. The bastard hits the ground hard, landing on his knees like the disgrace he is.

"I know the hierarchy is unstable right now," I begin, "but I'm not chosen to stand before our father. And this—" I kick Felix's side, making him yelp, "—concerns a matter of justice. I recently claimed a woman. Turns out she has freckles... *all over.*" I say it through gritted teeth. "Felix was her Guardian Angel."

"She's just a dirty slut!" Felix spits. "Mortals are *beneath* us!"

Orcus lets out a long, exaggerated gasp. "Did he *just*—Azrael, boss, you'd better kill him fast because I am about to commit a war crime."

Azrael doesn't hesitate. He swings Orcus down with a sickening crack, blade slicing through the air so close to Felix's hand that it sends visible shivers down his back.

"The fact that you missed pisses me off," Orcus hisses, vibrating with blood-lust. "I demand a redo. A decapitation. Something cinematic."

Azrael snarls, stepping closer. "You do realize saying that aloud just sealed your fate, right? You *will* face termination. My mate, your Queen, is half mortal!" He nods toward Sadie, who winks and waves like she's welcoming guests to brunch. "And she's the Sandman's mate. Your views? They're outdated."

I bow. Not for him. Not because I like him. But because Azrael is above me in rank—and one day, he'll rule the Underworld.

"How would you like this handled?" Azrael asks, cold and calculating now, like a blade sheathed in snow.

"He failed her. She was molested repeatedly. Mortal men... and *him*." I jab a finger at Felix, who tries to crawl away, shaking. "He didn't protect her. He *used* her."

Orcus hums like a lullaby, dark and slow. "Oh, ohhh. May I suggest dismemberment over a few days? I'll narrate. I have monologues ready."

"He failed to protect her! She was raped numerous times by *him*! I want a *slow* and *painful* death," I say simply.

Azrael nods. "Then slow and painful it is."

Felix screams. Orcus sings. And I don't feel a single drop of guilt.

Chapter Seventeen

Wynne

After Dark - Mr. Kitty

Whatever the hell an ogre rave is, I'm one thousand percent here for it.

The green lights are strobing like we're in Shrek's fever dream, bouncing off my porcelain skin and casting this weird, radioactive glow over the sea of sweaty, bouncing cartoon characters. Somebody dressed as a slutty Scooby-Doo just shotgunned a neon drink and I think I saw a Care Bear grinding on a minotaur. So yeah. Chaos.

I'm pressed up against one of the guys Nadia brought with her, and listen—I'm not complaining. He's tall, with caramel skin and long hair that brushes his shoulders like some kind of Greek god that discovered good conditioner. His brown eyes catch the light in a way that almost makes them look red—but I'm ninety percent sure they're brown. Maybe. Hopefully?

He smiles down at me, and damn. It's a smile worth sinning for. Straight teeth. Sharp canines. I want to fight him just to ask who his orthodontist is.

Then he taps my shoulder.

I turn, heart pounding with bass and bad decisions.

He drops a little white circular pill into my hand.

I take it.

Why? Because this is escape. And gods, I need it.

Nyxian.

That's the problem.

He's all I can think about. It physically *hurts* being away from him. And it makes zero fucking sense. I barely *know* him. He's all shadows and fury and sin in a perfect body. Someone like him *shouldn't* exist.

But he does.

Nyxian is real, and I miss the way he looks at me like he's memorizing every inch of my soul—like if anyone touched me, he'd burn the world down without blinking.

And don't even get me started on the sex.

Oh my fucking God. The way he moved. The way he sounded. The way he made me feel—like I was something sacred and filthy all at once. I crave him. His warmth. His weight. The sharp edge of his want.

What the hell has gotten into me?

Nyxian, that's what.

He's in my head. In my blood. Wrapped around my heart like some unholy vine, squeezing and curling and refusing to let me go.

But do I even want him to?

That's the real question. Because as much as I miss him, as much as I ache for him, I don't know if I can see a future *with* him.

But I damn sure can't see one without him either.

I shake my head, trying to drown the thought as the music spins and the lights twist around me like a kaleidoscope on acid. My toes are tingling. My brain is floating somewhere above the dance floor. I look at the caramel stranger again and flash him a smile—trying so hard to be *just a girl* at a rave.

Not some horny redhead who apparently fucked death reincarnated.

Just me.

I need to snap back to full reality. That includes fucking strangers and pretending I know what day of the week it is. This is what *normal* people do, right?

He leans in. I touch my lips to his—soft, quick, desperate for distraction.

He pulls back and grins, looking at his friend before nodding. "Wanna get out of here?"

"Sure!" I shout over the bass drop.

He takes my hand. Nadia follows, still glued to the other guy like she's ready to ruin someone's life in a bathroom stall. The music fades behind us as we move deeper into the building.

Except... we don't head toward the exit.

We're not going outside.

We're going *down* a long hall, where another man waits. And this one?

He's beautiful. No—*inhuman*.

He stands in front of a massive red door like a painting come to life. Hair dark as ink. Eyes too sharp. Too knowing.

I slow my pace.

Something about him feels... wrong.

And suddenly, my escape doesn't feel like escape anymore.

"Password?" the guy asks. His voice is flat, expression unreadable beneath a messy curtain of blond hair that practically swallows his face.

"*Suceur de sang*," the caramel guy says smoothly, like it's a totally normal Thursday codeword and not French for *bloodsucker*.

I blink. Um. Okay. Red flag? Yellow? Chartreuse?

Also, why have I not asked for his name?

The blond guy doesn't say anything. Just opens the red door and steps aside, revealing another hallway that stretches into shadow.

Cool. Love that for us. Definitely not murdery.

"I didn't know clubs had secret rooms," I mutter as we're herded inside.

"Most clubs in New Orleans do," caramel guy replies with a grin that makes me deeply suspicious of every life choice I've made in the past forty-five minutes.

Nadia laughs like this is *fun*. "So how do we find all the secret rooms?"

"Invitation only," he says.

I lean into her. "Where did you find these guys?"

She shrugs. "They found me at the gas station."

I stop walking. Dead. In. My. Tracks.

I look at her—*really* look at her—and there's a flicker of panic behind her glassy eyes. My own vision tilts sideways. My heart skips, then hammers.

What. The. Ever-loving. *Fuck.*

We are going to die.

"Hey, what did you give us?" Nadia asks, suddenly blinking like she's just now catching up to the vibe. "I'm feeling kind of... not okay."

"Sedative," he says. Casually. Like he just offered us mints.

A fucking *sedative?*

My chest tightens, breath stuttering. My limbs are starting to feel like they're filled with wet sand, and I can't stop thinking about Nyxian.

I should've stayed home. Waited for him. Fought for the chaos I *know* instead of wandering into this stranger-danger horror movie with rave lights and Scooby-Doo sluts.

I try to focus. *Okay. Okay. Calm down. You've seen crime documentaries. Breathe. Small talk. Stall. Buy time.*

"What's your name?" I manage, voice warbly and not at all cute.

"I'm Ski. He's Zach." He points to the one glued to Nadia. Zach looks like a steroidal garden gnome with a buzz cut and a nose that's trying too hard to be a personality.

"You didn't have to roofie us," Nadia slurs, still trying to flirt her way out of death. "We're 100% willing."

"It's so you won't be in *pain*," Zach replies.

He says it with a smile.

Then he tilts his head back—slowly, almost theatrically—and when he faces forward again, everything *shifts*. His skin pulses, veins are bulging across his forehead like something's trying to claw its way out. His jaw unhinges slightly to make room for the jagged, glinting *canines* that grow before my eyes.

Nadia gasps, her breath hitching like a record scratch, and takes a step back.

Too late.

Zach grabs her by the hair—hard—and yanks her neck to the side.

She *screams.*

It's a sound that rips through me. Raw. Real. Terrified.

And I run.

I don't think—I just bolt.

Yes, I left her. Yes, I'm a shitty friend. But survival instincts beat guilt every fucking time and I *am not* dying in a secret rave murder tunnel.

Except... Ski grabs me.

He yanks me around to face him, and I stumble, dizzy. His eyes—once warm and brown—are glowing red like the coals of a dying fire. A storm is building in them, and I know—*I know*—he's not human.

"Let me go!" I scream, thrashing like a fish caught on a hook.

It's pathetic.

I'm pathetic.

Zach sinks his teeth into Nadia's neck.

Her scream goes silent.

Just—*gone.*

"Help!" I shout, fighting to get loose. Kicking. Twisting. Trying to punch, but my limbs are Jell-O and the sedative's are slurring my strength.

"Help!" I try again, but it's not even a real word anymore.

Just a mumble.

A weak, fading whisper of a girl who made one bad decision too many.

And I think—no, I *know*—I'm going to die here.

CHAPTER EIGHTEEN

Nyxian

PAINT IT BLACK - VALLEY OF WOLVES

F or fuck's sake.

I step through the veil, shadows curling around my shoulders like a cloak as I land in a room that reeks of blood, rot, and regret.

And there they are.

My Little Disaster, slumped and fighting to stay upright, and her friend—Nadia—barely breathing, slumped against the wall like a broken marionette. Blood soaks her shirt, and her pulse flutters weakly in her throat. Wynne's eyes lift just enough to find me, drugged and dull, but burning with recognition.

Good girl. You held on.

But the sight in front of me? *Unforgivable.*

Vampires.

Fucking *vampires.*

Low-grade supernatural parasites. Mortal-born leeches who think that the dark makes them powerful. Who think drinking blood makes them kings.

I clench my jaw and let the fury boil up. I welcome it. Feed it.

The blonde one is still crouched over Nadia, fangs out, his mouth and chin slick with her blood. That's not just a bite. That's a fucking feast.

I don't hesitate. My shadows lash out like wolves off the chain, slamming into him with bone-crushing force. He hits the opposite wall with a wet *crack*, leaving a dent behind as he slides to the ground in a twitching heap.

The other one is gripping Wynne by the arm, his fangs hovering at her throat like he's about to carve his initials into what *belongs to me*.

Not today, fucker.

I lunge forward, grabbing him by the throat. His eyes widen just before I slam him into the stone wall so hard his skull bounces like a dropped melon. Then again—*crack*—and again. I don't stop until his body goes limp.

I throw him like trash, letting him crash beside his blonde friend, who's already choking on a collapsed lung.

The rest of the coven starts to slither from the shadows. More figures, more glowing eyes. Half-starved freaks, dressed like goth club kids from 2007. Twelve of them. Maybe fifteen.

I step between the girls and them. Casual. Controlled. A predator just stretching his limbs.

They freeze when they see me. My shadows coil at my feet like snakes waiting to strike.

"You have no business here, Reaper," the tawny one wheezes, blood dribbling from his nose as he struggles to his feet.

"The redhead belongs to me," I snarl, and whip a ribbon of shadow across the room. It slams him back down, leaving a spiderweb of cracks in the wall behind his head.

"Then the other one is free for the taking. Take what's yours and go," he growls, trying to rise again.

"I'd love to leave with just her," I say, half-turning to check the girls. Nadia is out cold. Wynne is still conscious—barely—her eyes half-lidded but locked on mine. Good. Stay with me, baby.

I turn back to them, a grin crawling across my face. "But you *touched* what's mine. And that? That means you die. No hard feelings."

He spits blood. "We didn't know a redheaded mortal would belong to a Reaper!"

"Too late."

I raise my hand slowly. Shadows answer like obedient beasts. They slither up his legs, across his chest, until two whip-thin tendrils wrap around his jaw.

One on the top. One on the bottom.

"Let's see if your kind still talks this much when I pull the fucking words out of your throat."

I yank my hand down—slow. Deliberate.

The shadows pull in opposite directions, stretching his mouth wider... and wider... until the corners split. A wet tearing sound cuts through the room as his jaw unhinges. Skin and muscle stretch like taffy, then *pop*—the mandible snaps loose. He lets out a gurgling scream as blood pours down his shirt, his tongue lolling from a now grotesquely open maw.

The rest of the coven panics.

They turn to run. Cowards.

But I'm not done.

The blonde little freak who touched Nadia, tries to slip into the shadows. Not on my fucking watch.

I flick a single thread of shadow—razor thin, singing through the air.

It slices clean through his neck.

His head tumbles forward, mouth still twitching. The body folds seconds later, collapsing in a heap of useless meat.

I exhale slowly, letting the rage settle just beneath my skin.

Then I walk to the girls.

One on each shoulder. Wynne melts against me, weak but safe. Nadia doesn't stir.

I step into the shadows and drag us back to her room—her sanctuary.

I lay them gently on the bed, careful not to wake either of them too harshly. Wynne murmurs my name once, and I swear, my entire chest fucking aches.

I brush the hair from her forehead and retreat to the dark chair in the corner. I sit there. Watching. Listening. Making sure they're breathing.

Then I check my watch.

There's more work to do.

Felix.

I rise, letting the shadows curl around my limbs again, swallowing me whole as I drop into the execution chamber of the Underworld. Red light bleeds across black marble. A crowd stands witness.

Azrael greets me with a tilt of his head. "Everything okay?"

"Dumbass met a vampire coven. She was drugged, but she's fine now." I brush past him and walk toward the platform where Felix is bound.

The bastard is already a mess.

One wing missing—i tore it off earlier like a chicken leg. His fingernails are gone, his big toes are sawed off. Blood soaks his skin in dried layers, crusted black and red. He's trembling, his breath wet and ragged.

Still alive. Barely. But alive.

And still defiant.

He lifts his face toward me, grinning with split lips. "Your whore tasted so sweet," he rasps. "She had a cute little whimper when her uncle was fucking her."

My hand wraps around his throat tightly.

I squeeze until his eyes bulge, until the veins in his face turn purple, until he starts to choke on his own smugness.

Then I summon a thread of shadow and slide it into his eye socket.

Slowly.

I twist.

He screams—raw and primal—and I drink it in.

The eye comes loose with a sticky, sucking sound, nerve endings stretching like wet strings before finally *popping* free.

I let the orb dangle by the optic nerve, his head jerking like a puppet.

Now *that's* remorse.

And we're just getting started.

Azrael turns to the crowd—an arena packed with angels, fae, and their wide-eyed children. Parents always bring their fucking spawn to these kinds of events, hoping the blood and screams will scare them straight. A nice little Underworld PSA: Obey the laws or end up like the sorry bastard choking on his own shadows.

"Take this as a warning," Azrael says, his voice booming through the arena like thunder cracking across stone. "Guardian Angels are not to engage in any unconsented relations with their charges. It is punishable by death."

He was born for this—commanding attention, wearing the weight of leadership like it was made for him. Crownless, but unmistakably a king.

Then he turns to me and nods.

The signal to end it.

But I'm not done.

I want Felix to die slowly. I want every second of his life to end in agony, knowing his last breath was stolen—not granted.

I let my shadows slither into his nose and mouth, winding deep into his lungs like smoke with purpose. His remaining eye bulges. His body convulses. He claws at his throat in blind panic, scraping his own skin raw as he suffocates on nothing.

His lips stretch open in a silent scream, lungs filling with shadows instead of air.

And then... he *stops*.

Still. Lifeless. Weak.

Disgusting.

I turn and leave the arena, my boots echoing in the silence left behind.

Azrael catches up with me at the edge, dragging a blonde woman behind him—small, delicate-looking, but I can feel the power rolling off her like a storm. A hybrid. Must be Layla. She wreaks of a mortal vanilla scent with something else I can't make out. Something strong and unfamiliar.

"What are your plans," Azrael asks, "if your mortal woman accepts the mating bond?"

I haven't thought that far ahead.

Would I bring her here? Let her live in the Underworld, surrounded by death and duty?

Or would I let her keep pretending she's normal, watching everyone around her age and die while she stays young? While she watches the world decay in slow motion?

"I don't know yet," I mutter.

Azrael studies me. "I'd consider moving her here. When I dethrone Hades, I want you on my council."

I arch a brow. "And what makes you think I'd ever serve under *your* Hierarchy?"

Layla, mouse-voiced and way too soft for this world, speaks up. "We could use you as a trainer."

I snort. "What about Exu?"

"He wants to retire," she says. "He's thinking about following our werewolf friend to the mortal world. Living a normal life."

Of course he is.

Azrael cuts in again. "You were my first choice, Nyx. I know I haven't always been the brother you needed, but you're not happy as a Grim Reaper. You're dual-trained. You're *lethal.* You could help raise a new era of Reapers—shape something better."

My arms cross. "I want a big house. Wynne wants animals, but doesn't want to clean their shit, so I'll need staff. Maids. Servants. People to handle her chaos."

"Done," Azrael replies without hesitation.

"And a koi pond. By the water. I want peace when I'm not dragging souls to their doom."

They both blink.

Then Azrael shrugs. "Done."

He turns to leave.

"Hey, Az," I call.

He glances back, icy blue eyes like sharpened glass. "Yeah?"

"Is this really what you wanted to be? A Reaper? Are you happy?"

"No one's happy with the work they *have* to do," he says quietly. "But we're rewriting the laws. Rebuilding the Hierarchy. And we want you to be part of that."

Then he walks away, cloak snapping behind him like the beat of war drums.

CHAPTER NINETEEN

Wynne

TAKE WHAT YOU WANT - POST MALONE FT OZZY OSBOURNE

I feel disoriented. Groggy. My head is pounding, and my body feels like it was run over by a semi. I try to focus my eyes, but everything's blurry, like I'm still wrapped in the fog of whatever happened last night.

Did I dream all of that? The vampires, the blood, the terror? But then there's the soreness between my thighs. Oh, hell no. I didn't dream *that*. Nyxian—God, I can still feel the way his hands held me, his presence, everything. That *wasn't* a dream.

I look around, trying to get my bearings. This room is familiar—my room—but something's off. The soft weight of Nadia's body sprawled across my bed pulls me back to reality. Her pink hair is a mess, and there's something darker on her skin—bruises, big and ugly. One's right on her neck.

So, I didn't imagine it all.

Everything actually happened.

The panic starts to crawl its way up my throat. What the hell did she get us into?

I push Nadia, trying to wake her. "Nadia." My voice is hoarse, but I don't care. "Get up, Nadia!"

She stirs, her pink hair falling around her face as she sits up, blinking like she's been hit with a truck. "What?" She mutters, still half-asleep, but then her gaze sharpens. "What the hell happened? Where are we?"

"I brought you here," comes a deep, dark voice from the corner of my room.

I freeze, heart skipping a beat.

How long has he been standing there?

I don't even have to look to know who it is. I feel him, like a storm on the edge of my skin. *Nyxian.*

Nadia's voice cuts through the thick tension. "Who the hell are you?"

I finally glance at her, but my gaze stays fixed on him. "He's Nyxian."

I know she's glaring at me, probably shooting me the *are you serious right now* look. And I don't even blame her.

"How did you two meet?" Nadia asks, her voice dripping with skepticism.

And before I can say anything—because I'm still trying to sort through the whole *I was drugged, almost died, and now I'm stuck in my own bed with a bunch of bruises from a vampire* thing—Nyxian speaks first.

"The night of the wreck."

Nadia's eyes widen, then she leans in with a dramatic swoon. "Oh? You were an EMT, huh? How sweet, trying to save lives in your off-hours."

"No." He answers, his voice as cold as ice, emotionless.

"Huh?" Nadia blinks, obviously expecting some follow-up.

"I took her soul that night and offered her a bargain." His voice doesn't change, but the weight of his words is enough to send a chill through the room. "Her love for immortality."

My stomach drops.

I look at Nadia—*great,* just what she needed to hear. Sweat beads at my forehead, a fresh wave of panic creeping up. I can already feel the shitshow about to unfold.

"Excuse me?" Nadia's jaw drops. I know she's still half-delirious from whatever sedative we were given last night, but I can already see the gears in her head turning.

"I'm Nyxian. A Grim Reaper," he adds, his smirk wicked and cruel. "Hello, Nadia. It's... *not* a pleasure to finally meet you."

That's *so* comforting.

Nadia straightens up, eyes flashing with irritation. "Dude, you can go fuck off! You're a psycho." She stands, probably planning to leave, but I see Nyxian's shadows twitch. Before she can even take a step, she's yanked back down, forced to sit on the bed.

My eyes snap to Nyxian. "What the hell, Nyx?"

"I've had enough of you putting Wynne in danger." His voice is low, and I can feel the raw fury in it. "You're a bad influence. After today, I hope I never see you near her again."

"Nyxian!" I scream. My hands clench, ready to throw something at him.

He doesn't move. His gaze sharpens, icy as always. "Enough, my *Ember of Life.* If I wasn't so attuned to your emotions when I'm away from you, you both would have been *dead* last night."

I freeze.

What?

Nyxian's gaze flickers toward Nadia, and in an instant, the shadows wrap around her, turning her head so I can see the ugly bite marks on her neck.

"She almost didn't make it," he continues, his voice steady but carrying a weight that suffocates. "Your grandfather says '*hey,*' by the way. He was waiting for you to come say your goodbyes—but you never showed."

Nadia blinks, tears filling her eyes. She looks like she's about to collapse under the weight of those words.

My heart drops. I can't bear to see her like this. She's been through enough.

"Nyxian, that's enough!" I stomp my foot, frustration bubbling to the surface.

Nyxian smirks, obviously enjoying my distress. "Temper tantrum?" he chuckles, leaning closer, the shadows swirling around his form like living smoke. "I'll *fuck* the tantrum out of you and leave you tied up until you can behave again."

"Fuck you!" I yell, but the words come out strangled, my emotions twisted into knots I can't untangle fast enough.

Nadia's eyes shoot to mine, wide with disbelief. I can see the confusion and fear in her gaze. I can't blame her. Nyxian—he's... he's not what I expected. But then again, I don't know what I could have expected. He's a Reaper. Cold, ruthless, and just as broken as I am.

No matter how terrifying he gets, it is apparent I can't run away from him.

"I couldn't say goodbye because I didn't want to see him at his worst," Nadia mumbles, her voice cracking. "PawPaw Charlie was a farmer. He always said the year he didn't plant his garden, we should worry. He didn't plant a huge garden, but he planted one. I spent time with him, drinking coffee, watching westerns, and just sitting in the backyard while the birds ate the seeds. That's how I wanted my last memory of him to be."

Tears fall as she takes a shaky breath. "I needed to get away because I knew I let him down, but I couldn't fucking stand seeing him hooked up to machines like that."

Nyxian's glare softens, but only for a second. He speaks quietly, the weight of his words heavy. "He just wanted to hear you say you loved him. One last time. I sat with him for hours, way past his expiration. He couldn't hold on any longer, Nadia."

Her face crumples as she looks down, tears streaming freely now. For the first time, I see something in Nyxian's eyes—guilt, maybe even regret. He glances at me, his eyes dark and voidless, but there's something there that makes me pause. He's... not as cold as I thought.

"You need to apologize," I say, crossing my arms, my voice firm. "You can't just walk around insulting people and acting like you're above everyone because you think you're a god!"

"I *am* a god!" His voice spikes, the shadows around him crackling with agitation. "Sorry! Sorry for yelling."

The room feels colder, the shadows lashing out, knocking things off the wall. He doesn't seem to care. "Nadia, if you don't change your life soon, you've only got a short time left. When I first found you, you had three weeks left... Now you've got three days until your expiration."

"What?" Nadia stammers, eyes wide with disbelief.

"You... have... three... days... left... to... live," he says, each word measured and deliberate. His tone is deadpan, like he's stating a simple fact, but the weight of it hits Nadia like a punch.

She looks back and forth between him and me, clearly losing her grip on reality. "I don't know what kind of game you two are playing, but I fucking hate it. And Wynne, I hate your new boyfriend."

"He's not my boyfriend!" I scream after her, but she bolts out of the room, leaving me standing there, breathless.

"Nadia!" I scream again, running to the door, but she's already gone.

I spin around, my gaze locking on Nyxian. "You didn't have to do that, you asshole!"

"Her life choices are affecting *you!*" He growls, his shadows swirling more violently. "I can't sit back and watch you throw your life away!"

"I am of no concern to you, Nyx! We're not a thing. We don't have a title. I am not yours!" I scream at him, my voice breaking, some of the words coming out hoarse and raw.

He stands up, slowly, like the world isn't moving fast enough for him. "You belonged to me the second you begged for your life." His eyes darken as he walks toward me, step by slow step. "This is your soul." He pulls a small vial from his pocket, the liquid inside swirling with a red aura, glowing eerily.

I freeze, my heart skipping a beat.

"You want it back? Do you want to cut ties with me? Because if you do, I'll be back—only then, I'll be doing my job. *The Reaper's job.*" He extends the vial to me.

I hesitate, my throat tightening.

"Go on, *whore*. Take it!" His words are sharp, cutting through the tension like a knife.

I lower my gaze, fighting the rush of emotions that threaten to overtake me. "You're so disgusting. You know that, right?" The words come out barely above a whisper.

"That's not what you were saying when you begged me to *fuck you*." His voice is a low growl. "And if I recall correctly, when you were in trouble, it was me you cried for. *Me!*" He slaps his chest, and the shadows react violently, bursting out like flames around us, consuming the room.

"I blame the sex," I whisper, he smirks and it is venomous.

I clench my fists, my pulse pounding in my ears.

"You can push blame wherever you choose, but just know this..." His voice is quiet, but the words sting. "As much as you're mine, I *belong* to *you*, Little Disaster." He steps closer, his breath coming hot against my skin. "I will *die* for you. I will give up *everything* for you. You're tired of working? *Fine.* I'll make sure you don't have to lift a finger. You wanted a beautiful house with land and animals? *Done.* I've got everything sorted, from the maids to the caretakers."

His words rush out like a dam breaking, the weight of them crashing over me.

He takes my hand, his eyes pleading with me. "You wanted a life with peace? I can give that to you. You wanted animals, but you don't want to feed them? I've hired people to do it. I'll fix *everything*. I just... I just can't think straight, Ember of Life. I'm trying to fix this, trying to get you to fall in love with me."

I stare at him, my heart racing, his eyes filled with raw, unfiltered pain. He's telling the truth. I can feel it in the air between us. But... I don't know him. Not really. And his world? I would imagine it is a nightmare.

"How can I love someone I barely know, Nyxian?"

The question hangs between us, sharp and biting, and for a moment, there's nothing but the sound of my own heart in my ears.

He holds his hand out to me, eyes dark but no longer empty. There's something in them now—something almost human. "Then let me *show* you," he says, his voice low, almost gentle. "Let me show you my world, my past... and the male I aspire to fucking be."

My hand hovers near his, the space between us electric. I shouldn't want this—I *know* I shouldn't—but I can't lie to myself anymore. I've been thinking about him constantly. Needing him, even when I swore I didn't. I missed him the second he disappeared.

I can take a chance on random guys in a bar—let them buy me a drink, kiss me, maybe even touch me—but the second they try to love me? I ghost them.

But Nyxian? He's not someone I can ghost. He *won't* let me. He just proved he can find me, no matter where I go.

This is a risk I've never taken before.

I can step forward—or I can shut the door and never look back.

"And if I don't like what you show me, Nyxian... what then?" I ask, my voice almost shaking.

"I'll leave you alone." His answer comes quickly, without hesitation. "I'll walk away. I'll let you make your own choices—no matter how much it fucking *destroys me*." He pushes his hand out further, offering everything and nothing all at once.

I look into those impossible eyes—dark, endless, like falling into the night itself—and something in me finally breaks free.

"What the hell, Nyx... just show me."

I grab his hand—and close my eyes.

CHAPTER TWENTY

Wynne

RUN TO YOU - BRYAN ADAM

I don't know why I thought this was going to be some calm, Netflix-docu-style montage with Nyxian flipping through moody black-and-white pictures. Of course not. Instead, he dragged me through shadows like we were late for a war—and my *skin* burned. Not metaphorically. Literal fire vibes. I fully expected to spontaneously combust like a marshmallow dropped in lava or something.

We landed somewhere that definitely wasn't Earth. The moon overhead was red—*red*, like someone slapped a filter on it—and it casts this eerie, blood-tinged glow over the land. Creatures moved past us, but these were not "aw, how cute" vibes. These were straight out of childhood nightmares. The kind you pretended didn't scare you while secretly clutching your teddy bear tighter.

I gasped, clutching onto Nyxian like a human seatbelt.

His shadows curled around me protectively, like a demon blanket. "I would *never* let anything hurt you, my Little Disaster," he said, and offered a smile that almost masked the pain in his eyes.

Almost.

He didn't slow down. Just walked like he owned this hellish runway, dragging me along by the hand. We passed pop-up shops—actual freaking *shops*—and non-human kids playing tag like this was the most normal Tuesday ever. What the fuck was this place?

And then I saw it.

No—*felt* it.

A mansion. Scratch that. A *mansion* that made every celebrity home I'd ever stalked online look like a glorified garden shed. Iron gates. Towering spires. Guards with serious *"don't-mess-with-us"* energy. Nyxian gave them a nod like this was casual, just another day in demonville, and led me along a brick path straight to the front door.

"To understand me better," he said, "you need to talk to the beings who've known me for over six hundred years."

I blinked. "You're *ancient*. Oh my God, I'm fucking an antique."

He knocked, and within seconds, the door opened. A man stood there with eyes like galaxies and hair so dark and streaked with silver, he looked like a walking dreamscape. And the *audacity*—he is so fucking gorgeous.

"Nyxian," he greeted with a warm smile. "Back so soon? This must be the mortal woman you've been raving about. Come in, come in!"

Raving? Me? Internally dying.

"I'm Ashton," he added over his shoulder. "Azrael! Gang! We've got company!"

We stepped inside, and I swear some gothic interior decorator from Pinterest sold their soul for this place. Everything was deep reds, stormy greys, and inky blacks. Moody. Dramatic. Kind of like Nyxian in a home form.

The dining room was massive. A long, obsidian table dominated the space, surrounded by people—some not quite people—chatting, laughing, and eating like this was a holiday brunch.

"What *is* this palace?" I whispered to Nyxian.

"The Underworld," he said casually. "Specifically, this is the Sandman's home."

"I'm sorry, the *Sandman* has a house that looks like Dracula married Martha Stewart?"

A laugh came from the table. "Just call me Ashton," he said, sitting beside a woman with wild black curls and a face so pretty it should be illegal. She elbowed the blonde next to her—another walking celestial event—and then turned to beam at me.

"Hi! I'm Sadie. That's Layla. The grumpy one over there is Azrael—he comes with a hunk of metal named Orcus. That hunk of metal," she pointed to another, "is Drepane. You've met Ashton. Sulky chocolate bar at the end is Exu. Gloomy angel is Vassago. That sparkly cupcake beside him is Song." Then she motioned toward a man bringing out a tray. "And *this* brilliant chef is Luca!"

I just stared. These were... *Are these dead people?*

They were eating pancakes and teasing each other like a sitcom cast.

The Underworld wasn't what I expected. No torture pits. No eternal screaming. Just a big gothic mansion full of monsters laughing like a damn family.

And I was the girl who got dragged here in flaming shadows.

"Azrael", I think that's what Nyxian called him, rises from the table like a king with a damn scythe and strides toward me. Tall. Intense. Gorgeous in a terrifying way. He offers his hand.

"You must be Wynne. I've heard quite a bit about you from my brother."

Brother? Oh hell.

He doesn't crush my hand, thank God—just firm enough to make it feel like he's scanning my soul for secrets. I try not to visibly sweat.

"I'm... I don't know what to say," I mumble.

Azrael smiles, and it's like a flicker of light through storm clouds. "Layla and Sadie were the same when they first arrived. You get used to it. Flo's around too—if you see a huge cat the size of a small car, don't panic. She's friendly."

A bubbly voice cuts in. "Mostly friendly. She likes to knock over cups for fun."

I turn toward the source: a woman with wild black curls, a killer smile, and a very visible baby bump. She looks far too cheerful to be standing in literal hell.

"I thought the Underworld was supposed to be, I don't know... terrifying?" I ask.

Sadie shrugs with a grin. "Some parts are. But mostly? It's like Halloween married a Bed & Breakfast."

Then she laughs—harder than I expect—and pats her belly. "But do *not* get pregnant down here. These little gremlins grow faster than mortal babies. I swear I blinked and suddenly I needed maternity leggings."

Ashton rises to help her up like it's second nature, and she waddles to the counter to fix another plate.

I glance at Nyxian. He hasn't said a word since we got here. His face is unreadable, his gaze glued to me like I might vanish. It's a lot.

"Come sit," a soft voice says.

Layla, the angelic one with kind eyes, gestures to the open seat beside her.

I nod, walking on autopilot, and sit down as Azrael sets a plate in front of me. "Coffee?" he offers, already half-grinning.

"No, thank you," I reply, trying not to sound like I'm about to have a panic attack.

He shrugs and returns to Layla's side.

I stare at the table, the silverware, the food. My brain tries to process this bizarre domestic scene in literal hell.

"So..." I start, trying to act casual and totally not terrified. "How do you all know Nyxian?"

Vassago speaks first. His voice is deep, smooth like espresso. "He's a little turd." The dude has fucking wings that are tucked in tightly to his back.

Exu reaches across the table to lightly smack Vassago's shoulder. "Nyx is one of the most impressive students I've ever trained. He was initially drafted into the army, but we diverted him. I made him a Reaper instead."

"Dual trained," Azrael adds. "Combat and death work. He's the only one who's mastered both."

"He was cast aside when he was young," Vassago says, mouth full of eggs. "Forgotten. But he grew into a male of his word. He's rough, but solid."

I swallow and look down at my plate.

Layla leans forward across the table, her voice like a soft blanket. "I was nervous at first too. I was scared. But supernatural males... they're different. They don't lie. They don't cheat. They don't hurt you—not intentionally."

She glances at Azrael, who offers her the kind of look that makes my stomach twist in jealousy.

"And," Sadie pipes up as she returns with a second helping, "supernatural male stamina is *definitely* a thing. Have you experienced that yet?"

"*Sadie,*" Ashton groans, dragging a hand down his face.

I open my mouth to respond but a new voice cuts through the room, dry and sharp.

"Excuse the mortal woman. She's a fucking idiot."

I blink. "Who the hell—?"

"That's the scythe," Sadie says casually, pointing to a shiny weapon resting beside Azrael. "He's a dick. I've tried to talk Azrael into melting him down and turning him into a decorative garden fence, but noooo, he won't do it."

"Because I have *tloyalty*," Azrael says without looking up from his toast.

I sit back in my chair, my head spinning. Shadows, ancient warriors, sarcastic weapons, supernatural stamina—this place is completely insane.

And yet... I feel weirdly at home.

Layla laughed softly. "Take it day by day. One thing I've learned is supernatural males are *patient*. But if Nyxian has his eyes on you? He belongs to *you* and you only. He won't just disappear and find someone else."

She glances at Azrael with a smile that makes something in my chest ache.

"He'll put himself in harm's way to keep you safe. He's wired to protect you... to satisfy you... to keep you happy."

I glance at Nyxian, who's casually sipping from a mug like none of this affects him.

"I can't speak for Nyxian since I just met him," Sadie adds with a wicked grin, "but sister, a *shadow daddy*? Whew! You should've seen him when he *killed* your Guardian Angel for taking advantage of you!"

The entire room goes still. All eyes snap to her.

"What?" Sadie blinks. "Was that a secret?"

"Sadie," Ashton groans, "I think you need to sleep. Go take a nap."

She shoots him a glare. "Listen here, *Sandman*. You put this parasite in me, so you're legally and spiritually required to tolerate the hormones."

I laugh—an honest to God laugh—for the first time since we got here. "What are you having? Do you know yet?"

Sadie's mood instantly shifts. Her hand drifts to her belly, and her whole face softens.

"A little boy."

She's glowing, absolutely radiant. I can feel the joy pouring off her. I glance back at Nyxian. He's watching Sadie quietly, then shakes his head and looks at me again.

"I still don't know you, Nyxian," I murmur, more to myself than anyone.

Sadie snorts. "Oh honey, just wait until you accept the mating bond. You'll *know* everything then. You get this weird telepathic connection—you can feel each other's emotions, see each other's dreams, all kinds of wild shit."

She pauses, then smirks. "I didn't know Ashton for more than a few *hours* before I fucked him."

Ashton chokes on his drink.

"That's enough," he coughs. "You *definitely* need to rest."

Sadie glares at him like she might start throwing toast. "Unless you're fucking me or rubbing my feet, don't you dare touch me, *Sand Boy*."

Then she looks at me again, all sass and sincerity.

"I only knew him for a week or two before he proposed the mating bond. One might say that I have that *gorilla grip* effect."

"The mating bond is unique, though," Layla adds gently. "It only activates if you *truly* accept Nyxian—every part of him. Who he is, what he's done, what he's capable of."

"And have *great sex* with their weapons," Sadie beams, like she just solved a mystery.

Ashton nearly chokes on his drink again. He looks like he's dying inside.

"Azrael had to fuck Layla *with* his talking scythe, so now she's basically in a committed relationship with two men," Sadie continues, completely unfazed. "And Ashton had to fuck me with his magical sand. Ten outta ten. Highly recommend."

Azrael shudders, actually shudders. "I don't even want to think about that."

"It was *great*, Death Boy," Sadie fires back, dead serious. "You should be proud. Your sand-throwing boyfriend has *skills*."

I blink. Just... *blink*.

Nyxian sips his coffee like this is the most normal fucking conversation in the world.

CHAPTER TWENTY-ONE

Nyxian

BROKEN - SEETHER FT AMY LEE

Being a Reaper is weird. It's like being in a massive, cursed family where half your siblings are strangers, and the other half are lunatics. You don't know them, but the second you do, you'd bury a body for them. No questions asked.

I glance around the table.

Azrael is a fucking idiot. But he's a rich idiot. Not just in coin—he's overflowing with love, loyalty, all that mushy shit I claim to hate. I hate how much I don't *actually* hate him.

He didn't question me when I dragged our brother to his doorstep to be exiled.

He didn't question me when I showed up again tonight—with Wynne.

No, the one asking questions is me. Why do I keep coming here? Why is it so easy to fall into this rhythm with them? I barely know these people, but they feel more like home than anything I've ever had. Why the fuck am I acting like a little brother who needs backup?

I glance sideways. Wynne's beside me, laughing—full belly, soft-eyed kind of laughing. She's relaxed now, or pretending to be. Either way, she looks good like this. Too good.

She shouldn't be here. She should be far away from this world, where nothing sharp enough to gut her is waiting around every corner.

But she's here. And I'm not letting her go.

Sadie slams her palms on the table, curly hair bouncing like it's got its own personality. "It's getting late. Why don't you two stay the night? No need in heading back when Luca makes a breakfast that tastes like it was blessed by whatever deity cooks in imaginary Heaven."

Luca raises a brow and offers a small, dark smile. I don't trust that smile. He smells like secrets and forest floor and something with claws.

We head down a hallway, Ashton leading us. The place looks like an old gothic manor—every door lined up like teeth in the mouth of a creature that's swallowed too many dreams. One by one, everyone disappears into their rooms. Azrael and Layla. Song. Vassago. Luca. Even Exu just nods once before vanishing behind a door with no words.

Ashton stops and turns to us. "This one's yours. Hope one room's enough?" He asks Wynne.

She opens her mouth to respond, but I cut in. "One room will suffice." I dip my head slightly. Formal. Respectful.

I used to look up to Ashton. Wanted to *be* him. Before I figured out I was never meant to be anyone but my own twisted, cursed self.

I open the door for Wynne. She walks in like she's entering a trap, and maybe she is. I follow and lock the door behind us.

She turns around with a wild spark in her eyes, yanks a pillow and blanket from the foot of the bed, and throws it at my feet. "You can sleep on the floor."

I look at the mess she made, then back up at her like she's lost her damn mind.

"You have jokes," I say dryly.

She blinks. Then her face shifts, like her brain finally caught the train her mouth missed.

Goldfish-brained bitch.

I roll my eyes.

"Oh... right," she mumbles. "You don't sleep."

"Correct." I'm already peeling off my jacket, because I've had a long fucking day and her attitude isn't making it shorter.

"You gonna watch me all night or something?" she asks, wary.

"Would that be so bad?" I cock a brow.

"Um, *yeah*. What if I fart in my sleep?"

I smirk. "You've already farted. Multiple times. Loud ones. Before I even existed to you."

Her face turns the exact same shade as her hair. Crimson. "Nyxian, I could have gone my entire life without knowing that."

She flops back on the bed and buries her face in a pillow.

Me?

I'm unbothered. I slide into the bed beside her like I belong there—because I fucking do.

I hook my arm around her waist and tug her closer, pulling her thigh up over mine so I can settle between her legs. Because I want her. Fuck, I always want her. Even when I shouldn't. Even when it would be safer for both of us if I didn't.

But I'm *not* safe.

And I'm *not* letting her go.

Because these beings will either help her solidify the bond or scare her away and I need to make sure I have enough memories to hold on to.

"Nyx, what the fuck are you doing?" She yells, wide-eyed as I slide closer.

"I want dessert," I reply calmly, like it's the most obvious thing in the world.

She jerks, trying to snap her legs shut. I catch the motion, rip the blanket off us in one fluid pull, and plant both hands on her knees, holding her still. My gaze locks onto hers, daring her to look away.

"Don't act like you're not aroused, Little Disaster." I smirk, voice dipping low. "I can *smell* it."

"I have a *problem*, Nyx!" she huffs, exasperated. "I get aroused by *anyone* looking at me the right way. I'm wired wrong. Of course I'm going to be a fucking *waterfall* when *you're* trying to wedge yourself between my legs!"

My jaw ticks, but I keep my voice even. "Then why won't you just accept the mating bond?"

"Because you terrify me!" she blurts.

I freeze. Not in anger. Not in frustration. Just... *pause.*

I blink slowly, her words punching through my chest like a blade laced in truth. "Why am I so fucking terrifying?"

I release her legs and shift back, sitting at the foot of the bed, knees pulled up, ankles crossed. I keep my posture calm, controlled, even when her words rattle somewhere inside my ribcage.

She pushes up to sit, her voice still sharp. "Because you're *so serious*, Nyx. All the time. Like you've got this iron shield around you that *never* comes down. You're *mean.* You're intense. You burn like hellfire and expect me to walk barefoot through it."

"There's more to me than what you've seen," I tell her, and my voice doesn't rise, but it hardens. "I can be funny. I *am* capable of sweetness. I can give you the life you fucking deserve."

How, though? How do I *become* soft when everything I've ever known is violence and vengeance? When all I've ever been taught is how to survive by keeping everyone at arm's length and a blade's length further?

"*Teach me*," I finally say. The words come rough, vulnerable in a way I hate. "Teach me what it means to be what *you* need, Little Disaster. I will learn. I *want* to learn. Just don't cast me aside for some mortal man who only knows how to keep your bed warm when I can give you *everything.*"

I slide closer, tone low but edged with steel. "I can protect you. Serve you. Provide for you. *Satisfy* you."

She doesn't say anything.

"Were you not satisfied?" I ask, more tightly than I mean to.

"I..." She hesitates. "I was, Nyxian."

"Then what's the problem?" The rejection slips into my bloodstream like poison. "Why am I not good enough for you, but those flesh bags before me were?"

She curls into herself, knees to chest. Her body trembles. She's scared.

Of me.

And yet... every time she shivers, her scent spikes with need.

It's intoxicating.

She's terrified of me—but her body still aches for me. *Craves me.*

I raise a brow and wait for her answer, but before she can speak, the *entire* house jolts like something underneath it exploded. The walls quake. The ceiling groans.

My instincts roar. I leap up, covering Wynne with my body, bracing for impact. I expect the roof to cave in, expecting to be buried in splintered wood and stone.

But nothing happens.

No collapse. No attack.

Just silence.

I lift my head, scanning the room, then slide off the bed and crack the door open to peer into the hallway.

Luca is sitting in the doorway of his room, legs stretched out like this shit happens every day. He looks up at me, deadpan, and mutters, "Sandman stamina. The house shakes when he *finishes*."

He groans like he's exhausted by existence. "Some days are better than others. I guess Sadie really worked him up today."

He shrugs, like this is the kind of information one casually drops over brunch. "There's coffee in the kitchen. Azrael'll probably show up once Layla passes out."

I squint at him. "What *exactly* is your role here, wolf?"

Genuine question. These superior males—Reapers, immortals, literal embodiments of power—and here's Luca, smelling like wet leaves and bad decisions, just *existing* among them.

He shrugs again. "Not sure. I just... vibe, I guess. I was almost sounded by a fae goddess once. That was interesting."

I narrow my eyes. "Saygin?"

His expression drops into something that's probably trauma. "How the fuck does everyone here *know* Saygin? Is she some Underworld rite of passage? Are you all a bunch of sick freaks?"

He buries his face in his hands, muttering to himself.

Honestly?

It's not the worst theory I've heard.

Chapter Twenty-Two

Wynne

Lost Cause - Billie Eilish

I roll over, groaning softly as I blink up at the ceiling like it just insulted my intelligence. The bed here feels like a rock, the air smells like ash and old secrets, and everything has this quiet buzz that makes it nearly impossible to *just sleep*. I miss my bed. My too-soft mattress, the plants in my window, and the coffee pot that sang me good morning like a loyal husband.

When I said I needed a *vacation*, this was not exactly what I had in mind. Note to self: next time, be specific. Less *"escape to somewhere different"* and more *"beach, cocktail, no vampires."*

I shift under the covers and let out a long sigh. The memory hits me: the whole house shaking like it was trying to break free of its foundation, Nyxian jumping out of bed like a protective maniac, and me? Apparently, I just... dozed off after. Because yeah, that's a normal Tuesday now, I guess.

There's no telling if it's morning or night. The windows are frosted, and the outside glows this weird hazy red—like hell got a filter. Is it sunrise? Blood moon? Am I in a fever dream?

My feet hit the floor and instantly regret it. *Cold*. Bone-deep cold that snakes up my legs and makes my teeth clench. I wrap my arms around myself, stepping into the hallway with the kind of slow, cautious pace that says, *maybe I'll turn back and crawl under the covers after all*.

Then I smell it.

Coffee. Real coffee. Not the weird Underworld blend that I would imagine tastes like haunted mushrooms. Does that even exist? I follow the scent, halfway convinced it's a hallucination, until voices make me freeze mid-step.

Nyxian. Azrael.

"It takes patience," Azrael says calmly, like he's hosting a meditation seminar.

"I don't have patience," Nyxian growls. He sounds like he's pacing, or maybe just vibrating with barely-contained rage. Classic.

"You need to learn it. Do you need more training with Exu?"

"No!" Nyxian groans. It's not even an angry growl—it's the sound of someone who just got asked to do group therapy against their will. "I've had enough of that prick in my life."

"Wow," a voice murmurs next to me.

I jump ten feet in the air, nearly yelping as I turn and find Exu—a literal fucking stealth god—bent slightly so we're eye-level. His smile is radiant. Smooth. That kind of celestial pretty that makes you want to confess your sins *and* ask for skincare tips.

"They know you're at the door," he says casually. "Come. Walk with me."

Still recovering from the scare, I nod and follow him into what I assume is the living room. There are bookshelves, soft chairs, and a fireplace that burns blue. It should feel homey. Instead, it feels like a room that *knows* too much.

We sit across from each other.

"Not long ago, I had a similar conversation with Layla about Azrael," Exu begins, folding his hands in his lap. "But theirs was a fated bond. Azrael didn't get to *choose*—it was written in stone. Nyxian, on the other hand..."

"He *chose*?" I ask, not hiding the disbelief in my voice.

Exu nods. "Nyxian was a loner. Never bonded. Never cared to. So when he proposed a mating bond—*of all beings*—it surprised us."

I frown. "I hate that word. 'Mate.' It sounds like I'm about to be bred like livestock or something."

Exu chuckles, rich and warm like aged wine. "Understandable. The term *does* carry primitive connotations. But here, it simply marks a magical bond. One soul tied to another. A commitment stronger than your mortal vows." He leans back, head tilting slightly. "It doesn't always result in offspring. It isn't about that. It's about *choice*. Loyalty. Permanence."

"So, like... magical marriage?"

He nods again. "The ultimate *'till death do us part.'* Except, you know... *actual* death."

"Yikes." I pull my knees up and cross my legs. "So, in your opinion—is Nyxian even *worth* it?"

Exu stares at me for a beat. I mean a full, unblinking beat that makes me feel like I'm being x-rayed by someone with a PhD in Emotional Bullshit.

"You're scared," he finally says. "Not of what he is. Not of his temper or the arrogance. You're scared he'll leave. That something will *happen* to him. That if you give in, you'll lose him."

I open my mouth—then close it. How the hell did he just...

He taps his temple. "My gift comes from the mind itself. Makes me a nightmare to spar with and a very good therapist." His lips quirk. "Wynne, our bonds do not allow for... 'divorce.' Once it is sealed, Nyxian *can't* leave you. He will crave you. Need to protect you. *Want* to be at your side."

I swallow. "But why *me*?"

"That," Exu says, rising smoothly to his feet, "is a question even he doesn't fully understand yet. But what he *does* know is that he loves you. Maybe in his strange, rough-edged, death-glare way—but it's real."

He walks to the front door and opens it, a flash of red light paints his silhouette.

"One step at a time, yeah?" he says without looking back, then disappears through the door like some celestial fairy god-uncle.

And I'm left sitting in this strange, magical house, feet frozen, heart pounding, thinking:

What the actual fuck was that?

"Wynne?"

The voice is soft, almost hesitant, but it still startles me enough to jolt out of my own head. I spin around like I've been caught stealing cookies.

Layla stands in the walkway, her arms crossed loosely over her chest, hair pulled into a messy braid like she rolled out of bed but somehow still looks ethereal. Not fair.

"You okay?" she asks gently, tilting her head.

"Yeah... I guess." I force a shrug, then frown. "Why did you accept your bond, Layla?"

It comes out of me like a confession. I don't even know why I asked. Maybe because Exu rattled something loose in my brain. Maybe because Layla's been through this and somehow came out the other side with her sanity intact.

She pauses. Her brows furrow slightly, like she's rewinding memories she doesn't always let play. Then she steps toward me and speaks with that quiet certainty only someone who's *lived* it can have.

"Because no matter what I did, I always found myself thinking about him," she says. "When I didn't feel safe, he made me feel protected. And not just protected... *seen*. I knew just by looking into his eyes that Azrael didn't have boundaries. So if I needed him, he'd be there. Always."

I chew on that, then blurt out the thing that's been gnawing at me like a rat in the attic.

"He doesn't scare you?"

Layla laughs—light but laced with something real. "Oh no. Azrael *terrifies* the fuck out of me." She exhales slowly, a wry smile curling her lips. "But not in the way you're thinking. He's not dangerous *to* me. He's dangerous *for* me.

Like, if someone tried to hurt me, he'd burn the world down before I even had time to blink."

I stare at her. At the ease in her posture. The truth ringing in her words. And something shifts in my chest—a bone-deep ache I didn't want to name until now.

"Nyx wouldn't hurt you either, ya know?" she adds, softer this time. Her gaze meets mine. Steady. Certain.

I blink quickly, as if I can clear my thoughts the way you clear your vision. Layla doesn't wait for me to respond—she just gives me that knowing smile and walks off toward the dining room like she didn't just drop an emotional grenade and casually stroll away from the explosion.

I stand there for a beat longer, watching the spot she disappeared into like it's a portal to another life. Then I finally move.

One foot in front of the other.

Step by step, yeah?

I follow her into the dining room—because maybe it's time to stop running from the fire and see what happens if I walk through it.

CHAPTER TWENTY-THREE

Nyxian

YOU DON'T OWN ME - JOAN JETT

"But the argument over coffee is redundant. It's bad for you!" Ashton groans like he's been personally betrayed by caffeine.

Azrael gasps, hand dramatically clutching his chest like he's been shot. "*Blasphemy!* I don't need this negativity in my life. We can't be friends anymore."

Then, with the flare of a theater kid who didn't get the lead role, he slams his hands down on the table. "How can someone obsessed with marshmallows hate coffee this much? Make it make sense!"

"It *clogs your heart!*" Ashton shoots back like he's doing us a public service.

Azrael and I both turn to glare at him.

"Oh..." Ashton scratches the back of his head like he just solved a really dumb riddle. "Right. I forgot. Grim Reapers don't have fucking hearts."

Why am I here?

This is the elite ruling body of the Underworld?

The Sandman, who thinks sugar is a food group.

The King of Death, throwing tantrums over bean juice.

And me—stuck in a sitcom I didn't fucking ask to be casted in.

We're fucking doomed.

A sweet, almost sickening smell hits me—bubblegum and something more delicate. Floral. Hormonal. I turn toward the scent.

Wynne enters behind Layla, and Sadie waddles in behind her, practically radiating third-trimester misery. She looks like she's one bad meal away from stabbing someone, but her scent? *Divine*. The hormones hit like perfume dipped in honey and heat. No wonder Ashton's been practically vibrating.

But it's *Wynne* I watch.

She moves slower than usual. Quiet. Her eyes flick to me, then away just as fast. Guilt? Nerves? I can't read it. I *hate* that I can't fucking read it.

She sits directly across from me. Azrael's seat. The one he just gave up like it wasn't an act of war.

Azrael notices the tension, too. He glances between us, then offers me a look—pitying and gentle. The kind of look I'd like to rip off his face.

Shove it, Azrael. Shove it so far up your ass you taste it.

"No progress on the bond?" he asks.

I respond the only way I know how—with a low, guttural growl. Wynne stares at the table like it's more interesting than any of us.

"I'll be taking her home soon," I say, voice sharp as broken glass. "I have matters to handle."

Azrael hands me a mug. I take a sip out of sheer obligation and instantly regret every life choice that brought me to this moment. The liquid hits my throat like warm tar laced with artificial suffering.

"What the fuck is this?" I cough, grimacing. "This is an insult to beverages."

"Probably s'mores coffee," Sadie chimes, rubbing her belly with the exhausted grace of a woman ready to give birth *yesterday*. "Luca left early, so he didn't make breakfast."

She takes one bite of the overcooked eggs and winces. "Who scorched the damn eggs like this? I *want* names."

Azrael and Ashton both point at each other.

"Azrael," Orcus rumbles from the wall, voice like gravel sliding off a cliff.

Sadie spins on him with the expression of a woman moments away from committing a war crime. "You. To. Hell."

Azrael, unfazed, shrugs and takes the seat next to me, chewing like he didn't just incite a hormonal rage.

Then, because he can't *not* meddle, he glances at Wynne again. "Don't be a stranger, Wynne. You're welcome here whenever."

Wynne just nods and offers a tight-lipped smile. No sass, no retort, no comment about how weird this room is. *Too quiet.* She's usually fire and vinegar. Now she's molasses in winter.

My brow lifts on instinct. Her heart skips—then starts to race. I can *hear* it, taste it even. Fear? Embarrassment?

Or worse... *guilt.*

I lean back, smirking darkly as I let out a chuckle low in my throat. The sound makes her jump slightly.

Good.

Let her squirm.

"What's so funny?" Wynne snaps, voice sharper than she probably intended it to be.

I raise an eyebrow, slow and deliberate. "Do you really want me to say it here?" I lean forward, licking the bitterness of this so-called coffee from my lip. "Or would you rather wait until we're alone?"

"Secrets don't keep friends," Orcus chimes in, voice like a damn gong.

I shoot a deadly glare toward my idiot brother's chatty blade. "Shut the fuck up, Orcus."

"Say it now, Nyxian!" Wynne shouts, her voice cutting through the air like a whip. "With your fucking chest!"

There it is.

The fire.

My wildfire.

I calmly set my fork down. Wipe my mouth with the napkin. Take a slow, torturous sip of the swamp water Azrael dared to call coffee. And then I speak.

"The fact that you can't make up your damn mind about the bond, yet every little thing I do—*every breath I take*—sends your heart rate through the roof. It fucking raises your blood pressure. Makes you fucking *wet*." I pause, smile against the rim of the cup. "You're practically soaking right now, *aren't you?*"

She gasps, scandalized, but I don't let her cut in.

"I've already fucked you into submission once. Had you begging—*begging*—for me to stay inside you. For just a taste, just a *sliver* of relief. So tell me, Wynne..." I tilt my head. "Do I need to fuck common sense into you next?"

Her skin flushes red—*rage* or *arousal*, it's a coin toss. But she's shaking. Everyone's dead silent. Not even Sadie's chewing.

I lean back, lips curving into a smirk. "My Little Disaster," I purr. "Give me *some* credit. You and I both know I'm not above crawling under this table and eating you out in front of everyone—just to show them what you *do* to me."

Her breath catches.

"And I've got a feeling," I add, lifting a brow, "you'd crawl under this table to suck my cock if I raised my brow at you long enough."

I wink.

That's all it takes.

She **launches** across the table, knife in hand, practically snarling, "You *fucker!*"

Ashton grabs her mid-leap, locking his arms around her waist. She kicks and thrashes like a feral thing. I don't flinch. I don't even blink.

Instead, I scoop another bite of eggs onto my fork, cram them in my mouth, and smile around the chew.

Sadie sighs dreamily. "Is this an enemies-to-lovers trope? Because this has me horny as fuck."

"*Take. Me. Home.*" Wynne snarls through clenched teeth.

I finish chewing, I swallow, and then I ask sweetly, "Don't you want to finish your breakfast first?"

"I said—*take me home!*" she screams, struggling harder against Ashton's hold.

I raise a finger, and my shadows coil up her legs like vipers. She's gone in a blink, swallowed whole and dropped straight into her mortal bedroom.

"You can sit in your room all by yourself," I mutter, popping another bite into my mouth, "while I finish this god-awful breakfast in peace."

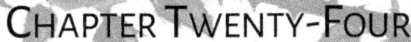

Chapter Twenty-Four

Wynne

Sweet Dreams (Are Made Of This) - Marilyn Manson

The darkness swirls like smoke laced with something malevolent. The dining room fades away, smeared and smudged like a half-remembered nightmare. My skin prickles—no, *burns*—as the air warps around me, shadows folding over my limbs like silk soaked in gasoline.

Then it snaps.

Suddenly, I'm standing in my bedroom, surrounded by framed photos of *him*. Nyxian. That smug, sexy, arrogant prick.

His stupid face is everywhere. Leaning against doorframes. Sitting on thrones. That devilish grin that looks carved by sin itself.

Oh, *hell* no.

I storm to the kitchen, rip open a drawer, and snatch a roll of trash bags like a woman possessed. My bare feet slap the floor as I stomp back to my bedroom, a whirlwind of rage and pettiness.

"This is fucking *insane*," I mutter to myself, grabbing the first photo. "Decorate my room with his face like we're middle school sweethearts? The fuck is this? Twilight?"

One by one, I start ripping the photos off the walls, slamming them into the trash bag like I'm taking out my enemies. Each *clink* of glass-on-glass is a tiny, satisfying victory.

Until I reach the last one.

I sit on the bed, holding it.

It's a candid photo—he's not even looking at the camera. Just slightly turned, that half-smirk on his face like he's always three steps ahead of everyone. His eyes are so black they swallow the light. Like staring into ink that's alive.

...Why *am* I being so defiant?

Yes, he's hot. Like, melt-through-the-floor hot. Yes, he can make me cum like a damn faucet turned all the way up. Yes, I wouldn't have to work a day in my life if I stayed with him. He's power, pleasure, and protection all in one annoyingly perfect, infuriating package.

So why does it scare the shit out of me?

I hurl the picture across the room with a scream. The glass shatters, echoing like a gunshot—and something in the air *shifts*.

Not figuratively. Not emotionally. *Physically*.

The barrier around me—my safety bubble—cracks.

I freeze.

There's a sound outside my room. A shuffle. Not like someone walking.

Like something *skittering*.

I rise slowly, heart hammering, and step into the hallway. It's empty. Silent. Too fucking silent.

The house doesn't breathe. It doesn't creak. It doesn't *live*.

I follow the sound. Step by slow, tentative step. Each breath feels like it echoes off the walls.

Then I see her.

"Nadia?" My voice wavers despite the steel I try to shove into it.

She's in my living room, hunched over my desk, clawing through drawers like a raccoon hopped up on bloodlust.

She whips around.

My stomach drops.

Her pink hair—usually bright and bouncy—is matted and clinging to her face in sweaty strands. Her skin is *gray*. Veins bulge from her cheeks and neck like roots from a dying tree. Her irises are bloodred, glowing, and seemingly *starving*.

Her *fangs* gleam.

My voice is a whisper. "Nadia..."

Her head tilts. "Where have you been?"

I raise my hands. "I've... I've been out."

She moves toward me—slow, but deliberate. "I've been looking for you." Her voice cracks, like something tearing inside her throat.

Every instinct in me screams to *run*, but I hold steady.

Barely.

"What happened to you?" My voice is shaking now. "You don't look like—"

"I'm *hungry*, Wynne." She takes another step. Her feet don't even sound normal. There's a drag in her gait, like her bones forgot how to move.

"But... burgers don't help," she growls. "I tried. I *tried*! But the hunger's still there."

Oh god.

Nyxian.

Where the fuck *are you?!*

How did I call him last time?

I try to think about him, to imagine his presence—*No*. Fear. I need fear.

So I let it hit me.

I let the terror rise, thick and drowning, and tears spring to my eyes—not from sadness. Not from weakness.

This is pure, fucking fear.

And she sees it.

"Oh, don't cry!" she coos. "It doesn't hurt. Not *much.*"

Another step. Her teeth glint like broken porcelain.

I step back. Now I'm fully out of the living room and in the hallway. My room is a straight shot. If I sprint, maybe—

No. *She's fast.* I remember how fast the vampires in New Orleans were. *Blurs.* Shadows. They could outrun cars if they wanted to. Do I even stand a chance?

I sob now, fully and raw. "It's me, Nadia... it's *Wynne.* Your best friend, remember?" My voice cracks and breaks.

"I was confused... I didn't know where to go..." Her lips tremble. "I came here for help... but you..." Her nose twitches. "You smell so *fucking* good."

She *licks her lips.*

"I'm just... *so hungry*, Wynne."

She lunges.

Adrenaline slams into me, drowning my fear in raw survival instinct.

I whirl on my heel and bolt toward my bedroom like hell itself is licking at my ankles. Behind me, I hear Nadia crash into a wall—hard. She shrieks, *"Fuck!"* and then her footsteps slam against the floor as she comes after me.

I lunge for the doorknob—but before I can twist it, she yanks my hair so hard my neck snaps back. I scream and crash to the ground, my knees burning against the cold floor.

Scrambling to my feet, I pivot and dash toward the front door instead, heart pounding in my ears.

But fate's a bitch.

I trip over a cracked metal candle sconce, one of the ones I had mounted to the wall—now lying shattered on the floor from when Nadia barreled through. My arms fly out to catch myself, but pain sears up both elbows as I slam down.

I gasp, choking on a cry. The world tilts, and I spin around, crawling backwards toward the door. "Nadia, please!" I sob. "Please don't do this!"

She stalks forward, bloodlust shining in her crimson eyes. "You just *smell* so fucking good," she purrs, licking her lips. Her tongue is gray. *Gray.* Like something decaying.

My vision blurs with tears.

Nyxian!

I scream for him in my thoughts, more desperate than I've ever been. *I'm scared! Please, please come. I need you.*

But he doesn't come.

Maybe he's ignoring me. Maybe this is the punishment—his cold shoulder turned into indifference. Maybe he's letting me suffer to teach me a lesson. Or maybe I'm going crazy, and he can't actually tell when I am in trouble.

Nadia grabs a fistful of my hair and yanks my head to the side. I feel her breath—ice-cold and wrong—brush against my neck.

My heart isn't just racing now.

It's skipping.

Panicking.

Fighting for a beat.

For a life.

Her nose presses into the crook of my throat, inhaling like I'm a feast.

"Don't cry," she murmurs, voice cracked and alien. "It doesn't even hurt."

I brace for the bite.

And then—

A crash.

Violent.

Loud.

A *growl* so low it rattles my bones.

Nadia's grip is ripped from my hair. I slam my eyes tighter and cover my ears, paralyzed by terror. Something wet splatters across my cheek. A sickening *squelch* follows—a gurgle, wet and horrible, and a final choking gasp that isn't mine.

I still don't open my eyes.

I *can't*.

Then...

A touch.

Warm.

Gentle.

A thumb brushing my cheek, smearing something sticky across my skin. Blood.

"My Ember of Life," a voice breathes, dark and velvet-soft, "when you call for me, I will *always* come for you."

Nyxian.

I snap my eyes open—and he's there. Kneeling. Staring down at me. His inky-black eyes are locked onto mine. Calm. Cold. *His*.

There's blood all over him—his chest, his hands, now smeared across my face. I try to look behind him, but he tilts my chin, forcing my attention back to him.

"No," he whispers, "just look at me."

His voice is coaxing, protective, and possessive in the most intimate way.

Tears spill again, but this time it's not just fear—it's relief. I reach for his face, pulling him closer until our lips crash together.

I let him kiss the panic from my body. I let him taste every goddamn tear I shed.

He groans into my mouth—a sound so guttural, it vibrates down my spine.

He lifts me easily, bridal-style, walking backward to shield me from the horror behind him. A shockingly thoughtful move for someone who threatened to eat me out under a table an hour ago.

His foot kicks my bedroom door open without pause, and he carries me to the bed, still devouring my mouth like I'm his *salvation*.

His tongue moves against mine. He tastes like ash and violence.

And I want *more*.

"I accept," I whisper, breathless.

Nyxian pauses, pulling back slightly, eyes searching mine.

"I accept you," I say again, firmer this time. "You scare the hell out of me, Nyxian... but not as much as the world I'm learning that fucking exists."

His expression doesn't shift—still unreadable—but I feel it in the tension in his arms. He's waiting. Processing.

I lean forward and reach for his belt, slowly unbuckling it. His breath catches, but he doesn't stop me. He doesn't even speak. But his fingers twitch at his sides.

I unzip his pants and slide my hand inside, eyes locked on his.

Still no words.

So I give him the only thing I have left to give—myself.

Keeping eye contact, I wrap my lips around his cock, taking him in slowly, savoring his salty taste. My tongue traces every inch, and finally—*finally*—his eyes flutter shut.

He groans again, this time deeper. His hips twitch. His hand fists the sheets beside me.

His walls are cracking.

And I am going to break every single one of them.

CHAPTER TWENTY-FIVE

Nyxian

THE OTHER SIDE - RUELLE

The way she sucks my cock makes it almost impossible to think.

Her mouth is warm, tight, and fucking addictive—and the way her tongue moves, the little gasp she makes when I twitch against the back of her throat—it makes every primal part of me want to *claim her* right now.

Right here.

Right through the mattress.

But a whisper of doubt slides under the heat.

Is she doing this because she *wants* to—or because she's scared? Because she thinks this is what I expect? I reach for her, fingers threading through her hair, and she *winces*.

I freeze.

She must still be hurting from when Nadia grabbed her by the scalp and flung her across the hallway like a ragdoll. I clench my jaw, bile rising. I should've gotten there sooner.

I try to move slowly, easing back into a rhythm. My hips shift forward with a gentler thrust, though it takes everything in me not to bury myself to the hilt. Her throat squeezes around me, and I can't hold back the groan that slips out.

I want to be careful.

I *try* to be careful.

But the truth is—I've never learned how to be gentle. Not really.

Not when all I've ever known is power, pain, and the satisfaction of control.

If we're being honest?

I want to break her.

I want to choke her until her vision goes dark, until her pulse stutters against my palm—and then bring her back with my mouth on hers, just so she knows I *own* her breath. I want to leave bruises she sees for days. Marks no one else could ever touch.

But I don't. Not now. Not when she looks up at me like *that*.

Tears streak from the corners of her blue eyes, glistening.

I pull out of her mouth, breath sharp, and lift her chin so she has to look at me.

"What's wrong, Little Inferno?"

She chokes out a laugh, wet and bitter. *"Everything."*

I blink. "Like?"

"Nadia. You. Vampires. The fucking Underworld." Her voice cracks as a sob escapes her. She wipes her face with the back of her hand, trying to shove it all back in.

Part of me wants to scoff. Roll my eyes. This is what humans do—they unravel at the edges the second reality tilts.

But another part of me... a deeper, quieter part?

Wants to hold her together.

"Then let's talk about it," I say, sitting beside her on the bed. My voice is calm, measured. It's too calm for the storm inside me. "Do you want to choose what to start with, or should I?"

She stares at my very naked body and groans. "Can you... maybe put some clothes on so I'm not distracted?"

I smirk. "You're literally the one who took my pants off."

I lean back, my cock resting against my abdomen like a challenge. "Stop deflecting."

"*Everything*, Nyx! Everything is wrong!"

"Okay. Vampires first." I fold my arms. "What about them?"

She sputters. "The fact that they *exist*! That's a good start!"

I raise a brow. "You've met Luca, right? The calm, brooding coffee boy? He's a *werewolf*. And they're more feral than vampires ever will be."

She blinks slowly. "But... he seems so *nice*."

I snort. "They all do. Until the blood takes over. Luca is a natural-born killer. It's buried deep, but it's there."

Her mouth opens, but I keep going. "And Nadia? She's not a big loss."

"She was my *best friend*." Her voice is so small I almost miss it.

I inhale slowly. "A best friend who tried to *kill* you. Let's not forget the fucked-up things she did. The manipulation. The sex. The drugs. The parties. The way she enjoyed it all and enjoyed stringing you along like an accessory."

"You didn't even *try*, Nyx. You didn't give her a chance."

"If I had, *you'd be dead*." My voice sharpens, cutting through the air between us. "I don't get to hesitate when it comes to you. I'm *wired* now to protect you. That's not something I can control."

"She was my friend!" she screams.

"And she tried to *rip out your throat*! That wasn't your friend anymore, Wynne."

"She wasn't herself—"

"She was never going to be again," I say, quieter this time. "That version of Nadia died the second she turned into one of those things. You know that."

I pause.

"I'm sorry," I say.

The words feel strange on my tongue. Foreign.

Her eyes fill with fresh tears. Her lips tremble as she stares up at me. That look—*gods*, that fucking look.

It's fucking devastating.

I can feel her pain like it's *mine*. As if there's some unseen cord between us, channeling everything she feels into my chest and wrapping it tight around my ribs.

"You don't mean it," she whispers. "I *know* you don't. You hated her from the start."

"I don't know what you want me to say," I murmur. My gaze drops to my hands. "I was just trying to protect you."

"You have to *know* when to protect me and when to back the fuck off," she snaps.

"But you *called* for me, Little Disaster." My voice cracks on the words. "You were terrified. I heard it—I fucking *felt* it. I dropped everything the second you screamed for me."

None of this makes sense.

She wanted me.

Needed me.

So why does she look at me now like *I'm* the monster?

What was I supposed to do? Let Nadia feed on her? Watch her die?

Nadia is the *reason* Wynne's been tangled in the extra drama to begin with.

She called for me.

So why does it feel like she's punishing me for answering?

I rake a hand through my hair, gripping it tight at the roots like that'll stop the ache building behind my eyes. I've faced warlords, gods, and worse—but this? *Her tears?*

They undo me.

"You think I wanted to kill her?" I whisper. "You think I enjoyed it?"

She doesn't answer.

She just looks away like I'm something she can't stomach.

"I didn't have a fucking choice, Wynne."

She finally meets my eyes, and the fury behind hers ignites like gunpowder.

"There's *always* a choice, Nyxian. You just didn't want to make the hard one. You took the easy way out—violence. Like you always do."

I flinch.

She doesn't notice.

Or maybe she does, and she doesn't care.

The worst part? I don't even know if she's *wrong*.

I swallow hard, voice rough. "I'm not good at this. I never pretended to be. But I need you to understand something—I heard your scream and nothing else mattered. I would've killed the whole fucking realm to get to you."

Her breath catches.

That makes her pause—but only for a second.

"I didn't need a killer," she whispers. "I needed my friend."

I open my mouth, but nothing comes out.

Because that word... *friend*... it doesn't fit in my mouth. Not when it comes to her. It never fucking did. Not when I've kissed her, claimed her, *touched* her in ways that make her *mine*.

"I'm not your *friend*, Wynne," I say quietly. "You *know* that."

She looks away again.

And that? That pisses me off more than it should.

I stand, pacing across the room, my hands fisting at my sides.

"I don't understand you," I mutter, half to myself, half to her. "You say you don't want me to protect you, but you *called for me*. You say you don't want the violence, but you fuck me like you *crave* it. So which is it, Little Inferno?"

She's silent. Trembling.

"I can't be everything at once," I growl. "Protector and monster. Soft and hard. Gentle and brutal. I don't *have* those layers. I only have *me*. And me?" I point to my chest. "I burn. I *ruin*. I protect by destroying everything that tries to touch what's mine."

She rises from the bed slowly, tugging the sheet around herself like armor. "Then maybe I'm not yours."

The room stills.

My blood turns cold.

I look at her like she just carved the words into my skin with a blade.

"That's not a choice you get to make," I say. My voice is low. Lethal.

Her chin lifts, defiant through the tears. "*Watch me.*"

Silence drops between us like a guillotine.

Something inside me snaps.

I cross the room in two steps, slamming a hand to the wall beside her head—not touching her, but caging her in.

"You *are* mine, Wynne," I say, barely above a whisper. "Don't lie to yourself. Don't lie to me. You know it. You *feel* it. You scream for me in your sleep. You call my name when you're falling apart. You *fucking beg* for me with every inch of your body when I touch you."

Her breath shudders.

"Don't stand there and pretend I'm just another monster. I'm *your* monster. The only one who gives a fuck whether you *live* or *die*."

She looks up at me, eyes glassy. Raw.

"You're right," she says, barely audible. "You are my monster."

She leans in, brushing her mouth against mine.

"But I don't know if I love you... or if I'm just addicted to the way you *break* me."

Then she walks away.

She brushes past me, and something in me *shatters*.

No.

No.

My hand shoots out before I even think—I grab her wrist.

Not hard. Not rough. Just enough to stop her.

Just enough to say *don't go* without actually saying it.

She freezes, her back to me. The air is thick, tense, and burning.

I step closer, lowering my voice to something softer, something that sounds almost like *pleading*, even if I'd never fucking admit it.

"You don't get to say something like that and walk away."

She doesn't turn around.

Her pulse flutters beneath my fingers, rapid. Unsteady.

"I'm not trying to own you, Wynne. I'm just..." I close my eyes. "I don't know what I'm doing. I'm not used to beings leaving. I'm used to them dying. I'm used to *losing*. So when I feel you slipping away, even a little—I panic. I grip harder. I fight dirtier."

Still, she says nothing.

I step behind her, my chest brushing her back, my voice low and torn. "I know I scare you sometimes. And maybe that should matter more than it does. But all I can think about is how I'd burn the entire fucking world down if it meant you were safe."

She trembles.

"Is that love?" I ask, my lips grazing her shoulder. "Or just the curse I was born with?"

She turns then—slowly.

Her eyes shimmer with something I can't name. Anger. Pain. Longing. *Me.*

"You think breaking me and protecting me are the same thing," she whispers.

"I think... I don't know how to separate them," I admit.

I reach up and gently tuck her red hair behind her ear, avoiding the sore spot where Nadia grabbed her earlier. My fingers linger against her jaw, and I can feel how hard she's trying not to lean into my touch.

"I want to be better for you," I murmur. "But I don't know what the fuck that looks like."

"It looks like listening," she says. "It looks like trusting that I can stand on my own... even if I choose to lean on you."

That gets me.

Because no one's ever *chosen* me before.

They've used me. Feared me. Obeyed me.

But not her.

She's chaos wrapped in vulnerability. Fire dressed like a girl. And when she looks at me like this—like I'm not just her captor or her savior or her executioner—I start to think maybe I *could* be more.

I press my forehead to hers, closing the distance.

"I'm trying, Little Inferno," I whisper. "I'm trying not to fuck this up."

She exhales shakily. "Then stop treating love like it's war."

I kiss her.

It's not like before. Not desperate. Not hungry.

It's slow. Raw. Almost hesitant.

And when she kisses me back, it feels like something *shifts*.

I pull away from her lips, watching her eyes flutter open—so fucking dazed, so fucking exhausted.

She tries to lean into me again, but I catch her chin in my hand, steadying her.

"Little Disaster," I murmur, brushing my thumb over the faint bruise at her jaw, "you need to rest."

She blinks up at me, her voice hoarse, barely a whisper. "I don't want to stay here. I'm scared."

It punches through me harder than I expect.

Fuck, her voice sounds so small. So unlike her.

I nod, once. Sharp. No hesitation. "Then you won't stay here."

I scoop her up into my arms before she can argue. Her arms automatically loop around my neck, clutching me tight. She doesn't protest.

That alone tells me how badly she needs this.

I carry her out of her ruined bedroom, stepping over Nadia's body without even glancing at it. I teleport us to Ashton's estate in a blink, shadows swallowing us whole and spitting us back into the moonlit foyer.

The house is dark and quiet. Good. No one needs to fucking see her like this... and no one needs to see me naked.

I walk us straight to the loaned room—*our* room now—and gently set her down on the bed. She immediately curls into the covers, small and trembling, like she's trying to disappear.

I sit on the edge of the mattress, brushing her hair back from her face, careful not to pull where it's sore.

"You're safe now," I say. It sounds stupid. Weak. But I don't know what else to give her right now.

She's halfway to sleep already, her breathing slow and uneven, her fingers still relaxing on my chest like she is scared that I will just fucking vanish.

I lie down beside her, keeping a small distance, careful not to crowd her. I keep my eyes on the ceiling, fighting the insane urge to pull her into my chest and chain her there so nothing can ever touch her again.

Minutes stretch by. The darkness grows heavier.

Eventually, she shifts, barely conscious, and presses herself into my side. A soft, broken noise slips from her lips—a sound of absolute trust.

I curl my arm around her, finally letting myself breathe. Finally allowing myself to just fucking relax...

CHAPTER TWENTY-SIX

Nyxian

MEDICINE — DAUGHTER

The dining room is dim, lit only by the faint orange glow of the lanterns Ashton insisted on stringing up.

The women are still asleep. Thank fuck.

I sit hunched over in one of the heavy chairs, a mug of black coffee cooling between my hands. The steam is curling lazy patterns in the air. Across from me, Azrael lounges in a chair like he owns the world, and Ashton leans casually against the wall. His arms are crossed, and he is wearing an unreadable look on his face.

None of us speaks for a while. The silence stretches, dense and weighty, broken only by the occasional tick of the clock on the wall.

Finally, I break it.

"I could feel her." My voice comes out rougher than I mean it to. I don't lift my head. "Not just hear her. I fucking *felt* it. Her fear... her pain... it was like someone drove a blade into my ribs and twisted it."

Azrael's dark brows lift slightly. He shares a look with Ashton. Something heavy passes between them.

"And you're sure it wasn't just... empathy?" Ashton asks slowly, watching me too closely.

"No," I snap, more harshly than I intended. I rake a hand through my hair, yanking the strands back from my face. "It was... *more*. It wasn't normal."

Azrael leans forward, his elbows resting on the table. "You said you heard her call for you?"

I nod stiffly.

"And you felt her fear like it was your own?"

Another tight nod.

Both Ashton and Azrael exchange another look, this one even heavier.

I take a sip of the awful coffee just so I don't have to answer right away.

Azrael raises an eyebrow, staring at me like I'm some kind of puzzle he's about to solve. "You ever wonder," he drawls, "if maybe you accidentally sealed the bond?"

I stiffen.

"No," I say flatly.

Azrael smirks. "You sure? Because it sounds like it."

Ashton tilts his head. "Alright, serious question—" he points the rim of his coffee cup at me, "—how many times have you two fucked?"

I almost spit my coffee across the table.

"Why the fuck does that matter?"

"Just answer the question," Azrael deadpans. "For science."

"For *science*," Ashton repeats, nodding solemnly.

I slam the cup down, scowling. "Twice."

Azrael and Ashton exchange a look like I just confirmed their fucking suspicions.

"And," Ashton says, grinning now, "did you use your shadows on her?"

I blink. "What?"

"You heard him," Azrael says, kicking a chair leg. "Did you use your powers on her? During."

"Define *use*," I mutter.

Ashton laughs under his breath. "That's a yes."

I shove a hand through my hair, scowling harder. "I didn't *mean* to. It's instinctual. It just... happened."

Azrael whistles low. "Yeah, that's a bond waiting to happen."

"Fuck off," I growl.

They're both laughing now.

"You don't get it," I snap. "It's not like that."

"Uh-huh," Ashton says, grinning so wide it's a wonder his face doesn't crack. "It's *exactly* like that."

I grit my teeth.

Because the thing is?

They're probably right.

I *felt* her. Felt everything. Every goddamn pulse of fear, every broken sob, every hitch of her breath like it was happening in my own body. And even now, sitting here?

I can still feel the slow, steady rhythm of her heartbeat just down the fucking hall.

Safe.

Near me.

Azrael leans forward, elbows on the table, smirking like he's won something.

"Congratulations," he says dryly. "You're halfway mated and you didn't even have to buy her dinner first."

Ashton laughs so hard he almost spills his coffee.

I flip them both off and shove my chair back with a loud scrape. "Fuck both of you."

Before either of them can snicker again, a low, measured voice cuts through the tension.

"The real issue here isn't the accidental bond," Vassago says, stepping into the dining room with his usual ghost-silent tread. His golden eyes lock onto me, full of sharp judgment and grim calculation. "It's the fact that a mortal has been tied to a Reaper accidentally. If others catch wind of this, it won't be Wynne they come after. It'll be you... because of you, other Reapers might start taking advantage of the mortals."

The atmosphere thickens.

Azrael's amusement disappears instantly. Ashton's easygoing posture tenses.

I frown, grounding my fists into the table. "Explain," I growl.

Vassago moves closer, voice smooth but cold. "Mortal and supernatural bonds are rare — but acceptable under certain conditions. Mortal and Reaper bonds? Never. *Never.* It's seen as...corruption. A weakening of death's dominion."

I turn to Azrael. "But Layla–"

"Isn't a mortal, per-say." He mumbles.

"Convenient," I snarl.

"It's not *convenient*," Vassago cuts in. His golden gaze flicks between Azrael and me, weighing the tension like coins on a scale. "It's a loophole. And it's one you don't have. Wynne is mortal. Mortal blood. Mortal heart. Mortal soul."

"And she's *mine*," I snap before I can stop myself, my shadows curling dark and fast under my skin.

Azrael watches me carefully, almost warily now. "You might think that," he says lowly. "But if the council catches wind of this... they'll think you claimed her soul. They'll think you're building something that could unravel Death's authority over the mortal world."

Vassago nods, voice like a scalpel. "They'll call it a Dark Claim."

The room falls into a heavy silence, broken only by Ashton's quiet exhale.

"You didn't just make yourself a target, Nyxian," Vassago says, stepping back toward the door. "You made *her* one too."

"But others have done it! So why would *I* be targeted if I made a mortal my mate?" I snap, slamming my palm down on the table hard enough to rattle the plates.

Vassago's mouth curls into a humorless smirk. "Because you're a Reaper, Nyxian. You aren't just a soldier of the Underworld — you're the enforcer of balance. Mortals fear you, obey you. If a Reaper starts choosing favorites... starts *bonding* with them..." His eyes gleam coldly. "It tips the scales. It undermines what we are."

Azrael leans forward, voice low, steady. "You think mortals could ever fear Death if they believed it could be... *seduced*?"

Ashton sighs and leans back lazily, but his eyes are sharp under the relaxed facade. "It's politics. Optics. Fear management."

I clench my fists until my knuckles crack. "I don't give a fuck about optics. She's mine. End of story."

"No," Vassago says quietly. "It's never that simple."

He steps into my space, close enough that my shadows hiss against his aura. "You, Nyxian, are dangerous enough without a bond tying your heart to something so fragile. To them, this isn't just about one girl. It's about what you represent. The precedent you set. If you can claim a mortal..." His gaze sharpens. "So can others. Chaos follows."

The air feels heavy, charged.

Azrael meets my eyes, serious now. "You need to understand... they'll see it as a Dark Claim. Forbidden. Corrupt."

"And if they decide to punish you..." Ashton drawls, tapping the table with two fingers, "they won't just come for you, brother. They'll come for *both* of you."

"Well, I guess it's a good thing Azrael is taking the throne, huh?" I deadpan, slouching back in my chair like I couldn't give less of a shit.

Azrael's mouth twitches, but not into a smile. "Don't think for a second I'll be able to protect you from everything, Nyxian."

"You won't have to," I mutter, cracking my knuckles. "*Let* them come."

Vassago's eyes narrow like a blade being honed. "You're not hearing us. This isn't some bar fight you can punch your way out of. If the Grim Council decides you've corrupted the balance, it won't be a battle. It'll be an execution."

Ashton exhales heavily, dragging a hand down his face. "And not just yours."

A dark pulse stirs in my chest, low and seething. "They'd go after her." It's not a question. It's a certainty.

"They'd *start* with her," Vassago says, voice low and brutal.

Something snaps inside me. My shadows crackle across the floor, a silent scream of violence that has all three of them tensing automatically.

Azrael watches me carefully, voice razor sharp. "Nyxian, control it."

I close my eyes, wrestling the chaos back under my skin. When I open them again, my voice is a growl. "Let them fucking try. Why didn't you warn me of all this when I first bought her here?"

"I didn't think she would be willing to bond." Azrael looks down at his hands.

Layla stumbles into the kitchen, hair messy, eyes heavy with sleep — but burning with something fiercer underneath.

"I won't allow them to hurt you or Wynne, Nyxian." Her voice is hoarse but steady, like steel dragged through fire. "If you don't have faith in anything else—" she plants her hand firmly on the table, staring straight at me, "—believe you can have faith in me."

The room falls dead silent.

Even Vassago, who usually has some cold remark locked and loaded, closes his mouth.

Azrael's gaze snaps to her like she just shifted the earth itself. "Layla—" he starts, but she cuts him off with a sharp look.

I stare at her, thrown off balance for the first time in a long fucking time.

Faith?

In anyone but myself?

In her?

The shadows coiling under my skin slow.

Layla moves closer, her expression fierce enough to almost look like one of us — not a mortal, not even whatever-the-hell she is now — but a goddamn force. "You're not alone anymore, Nyxian. Stop acting like it."

I open my mouth, but nothing comes out. For once, I have no idea what the fuck to say.

Azrael's jaw tightens, his gaze flickering between Layla and me. His protective instincts flare, and I can almost hear the unspoken words — the *"You're putting her in danger"* echoing between us. But Layla, ever the storm that she apparently can be, stands firm. She's not just holding her ground; she's claiming it.

I notice the way her posture has changed, like a mantle of power resting on her shoulders, despite the exhaustion still clouding her features. It's as if she's daring anyone to challenge her.

Azrael steps forward, his voice low, carrying the weight of a king's warning. "Layla, this is more complicated than you realize. Nyxian—" He glances at me, but I don't need him to finish the thought. I already know where this conversation is going.

I give a slight, almost imperceptible shake of my head, locking eyes with him. The idea that I could be something to Wynne, that this bond — this damn dark claim — could be my mistake, something that can be erased by killing us both... It's too much. The weight of that thought sits heavy in my chest. But for the first time in what feels like forever, I don't feel like I'm sinking under it alone.

Layla's voice breaks through the silence again, sharper than I expected. "I'm not asking for your approval, Azrael. I'm not asking *anyone's* approval. But what I *am* saying is this: if anyone tries to touch him, or Wynne—" She turns her gaze toward me, a flash of fire lighting her emerald eyes that might have scared the hell out of anyone else. "—you'll have to go through me first."

I blink at her, feeling a strange heat bubble beneath the surface. She's not just defending me — she's taking charge of the entire goddamn battlefield.

And something in me... something deeply rooted in me, something I've tried to bury... fucking admires it.

Vassago steps closer, crossing his arms and tilting his head. "Interesting," he mutters, eyeing the two of us like we're an equation he's trying to solve. "A mortal claiming a Reaper... a Reaper... claiming a mortal. I don't know if you'll have the chance to see it through, Nyxian."

Azrael sighs, his gaze softening just a touch as he watches Layla, but still filled with concern. "You're serious, aren't you? About this... this bond." His words are carefully measured, cautious. It's clear he's weighing the risks of all of this — for Layla, for me, for Wynne.

For the first time, I find myself nodding. "I am," I say quietly. "I'm not letting her go."

Azrael meets my eyes for a long moment, then exhales slowly, as though resigning himself to something he can't change. He turns to Layla, a touch of exasperation mixed with respect in his voice. "You have no idea what you're getting involved in, do you, Mouse?"

She meets his stare without flinching. "I don't need to. I'm already in it. And now, so are you. You are all big talk about me being Queen of the Underworld and the Grim Court fears me. I won't let them touch Nyxian."

Azrael opens his mouth, but no words come out for a moment. It's as if Layla has just knocked the breath out of him. There's a flicker in his eyes, something I can't quite place, and for the first time, he looks uncertain.

I can see the conflict in him, the weighing of the decision. Layla isn't just his mate or his equal in the council now — she's something else entirely. She's a force unto herself, a tide that pulls the Underworld's entire politics in a direction it's never been before.

Vassago tilts his head slightly, his eyes narrowing with interest. "You think you can change things that much, Layla? You think the Grim Court will listen to you? You're a —" he adds, his voice carrying a bite of skepticism.

Layla steps forward, crossing the distance between them in three short strides. "I don't think. I *know*." Her voice doesn't waver, not even a little. It's full of conviction, a sharp contrast to the quiet, simmering tension in the room.

"Maybe you should start listening, Vassago," she says, her gaze hardening. "I've heard your opinions before. But it's time to move past this '*mortal*' nonsense. The truth is, you're just as afraid of change as everyone else in this room."

There's a silence. The kind that presses down on everything, heavy and suffocating.

I'm still standing there, watching this exchange unfold. I thought I understood how Layla worked — how she moved and spoke, how she fought for what was hers. But this... this is different. She's not just protecting me. She's putting herself in the line of fire for something much bigger. For the entire Underworld.

Azrael finally exhales, pushing a hand through his hair, his posture loosening just slightly. "I don't have time for this. I'm trying to protect him, Layla. And you—" He looks to me then, his eyes flicking to mine. "You need to be careful. We're talking about the balance of the entire Underworld here. One wrong move, and..."

"I'm not just doing this for me," I say, cutting him off. My voice feels like gravel in my throat, but I need him to hear me. "I'm doing this for Wynne. I don't care what anyone *else* thinks."

Vassago lets out a low chuckle, an edge of amusement in his voice. "And you, Nyxian? You're willing to risk it all? To *embrace* possible termination?"

I meet his eyes, the challenge between us clear. "*Yes.*"

"Then you've truly gone mad, haven't you?" Vassago shakes his head, but there's a hint of respect there, buried under his cynicism. "I never thought I'd see the day when you, Nyxian, the fucking unbreakable, the gods damned untouchable... would willingly shackle yourself to something like *this*."

"It's not a shackle," I growl, stepping forward. "It's a *choice*."

For a moment, the room falls into an eerie silence again. Everyone seems to be holding their breath, waiting for something to crack. Waiting for me to back down.

But I won't.

Layla steps closer to me, her hand brushing against mine, grounding me in a way I couldn't imagine she could. Her emerald eyes find mine, a silent promise passing between us. She's right. We're all in this together, for better or worse.

And no one—*no one*—will take this from Wynne and me. Not now, not ever... and I *wish* a motherfucker would try.

CHAPTER TWENTY-SEVEN

Wynne

DANGEROUS WOMAN - ARIANNA GRANDE

The sunlight filters softly through the curtains, casting a warm glow over the room. I stir, the remnants of yesterday's chaos still heavy in my mind. It's strange how the night feels like a fever dream — fuzzy around the edges but still clawing at my ribs. Nyxian, with his broody shadows and "I'm too good for sleep" attitude, lingers in my thoughts like a bad tattoo. A reminder that I'm not just some clueless human caught in a world I don't understand anymore. No, lucky me — I'm part of it now. Front-row seat to the apocalypse.

I rub my eyes and groan, swinging my legs over the edge of the bed. Everything hurts. Muscles I didn't even know existed are staging a rebellion. The bed beneath me is stupidly comfortable, and yet here I am — still one mental breakdown away from chewing on drywall.

I sit there for a moment, debating if it's worth it to face the circus waiting outside. Pretty sure I'm not even remotely ready for human interaction — or, you know, death personified interaction — but my stomach votes *yes*. Loudly.

The room is quiet except for the soft rustling of fabric, and when I blink through my morning brain fog, I realize Nyxian is nowhere in sight. Of course he's not. Sleep is for the weak, and apparently, reapers with jawlines that could cut glass refuse to rest.

Rolling my eyes, I haul myself up and shuffle toward the hallway. The scent of brewing coffee and something savory hits me like a freight train. *Bless whoever is responsible for that.* My stomach growls again, louder this time, because it has zero chill.

I step into the dining room, half expecting to find a demon brawl or some sort of existential crisis in progress, but instead I'm greeted by... the *family breakfast special.*

Azrael sits at the head of the table looking like he walked out of a 'GQ: Death Edition' spread, his gaze so intense I'm surprised the walls don't catch fire. Layla's beside him, her warm smile trying (and almost succeeding) to make up for the emotional black hole next to her. Luca's at one end, looking criminally attractive for someone I'm 99% sure has a body count. Vassago lounges nearby, wearing a smirk that screams *I know more than you and I'm not sorry about it.*

Sadie and Song are tucked together, chatting away. Sadie spots me immediately and waves like we're about to swap friendship bracelets, while Song offers me a quiet, knowing smile.

Ashton, of course, is doing his best "too cool for school" lean against the wall, arms crossed, looking like he's two seconds from dropping some cryptic wisdom and disappearing into the mist.

And then there's Nyxian.

Already seated, posture so perfect it's *offensive*, like he's posing for a dark academia portrait. His eyes find mine instantly, and it's *game over*. My brain does a graceful swan dive straight into the gutter.

Because the way he's looking at me?

Yeah.

If he asked, I'd let him toss me over this table and ruin me without a single ounce of shame.

Get it together, Wynne.

"Good morning," I mumble, trying to sound casual and failing spectacularly. My voice is scratchy, like I spent the night screaming into a void — which, honestly, would track.

Luca turns with a gentle smile that immediately drops my anxiety from a Level 9 to a respectable Level 6. "Morning," he says, like I'm just another normal person and not a ticking time bomb of trauma.

Sadie grins and waves her fork at me. "You look like you need food. I know I do. *Starving.*" She shovels a mountain of eggs onto her plate like the relatable queen she truly is.

Song smiles at me sweetly, her silver eyes twinkling. Honestly, if Song told me the world was ending, I'd probably just nod and ask if she wanted to grab coffee first.

I hover awkwardly for a second, then force myself forward. Every step feels like walking into enemy territory, but hey, when has that ever stopped me before?

Nyxian's eyes never leave me. It's like he's pinning me to the earth with just his stare, daring me to falter. I don't — mostly because my stubbornness is stronger than my fear.

I drop into the seat across from him, trying not to look as rattled as I feel. Spoiler alert: I'm totally fucking rattled.

The silence stretches. It's not exactly hostile, but it's *loaded*. Like everyone's waiting for the gun to go off.

Vassago, never one to waste a perfectly good opportunity to stir the pot, leans forward lazily. "So, how do you feel, little mortal? Adjusting well to your new life?"

His tone is silk wrapped around a dagger, and honestly? I'm too tired to care.

I flash him a bright, fake smile. "Living the dream, obviously. Thinking about sending out some 'Wish You Were Here' postcards later."

Vassago chuckles, the sound dark and amused. "Touché."

Azrael's voice cuts through the banter, low and rumbling. "Enough, Vassago. We're not here to play games." His gaze flicks to me, a little less murdery than usual. "If you need anything, Wynne, don't hesitate to ask."

I nod quickly. "Thanks. I'll let you know if I spontaneously combust."

Nyxian shifts in his seat, a barely-there movement, but it feels like the entire room tilts because of it. His gaze sinks deeper into me — heavy, dark, full of things I'm not ready to name yet.

And for a second — just a second — I forget how to breathe.

Nyxian's gaze sharpens, like he's made some kind of decision in that dark, broody head of his. He leans forward, resting his forearms on the table, the veins in his hands flexing ever so slightly. His voice, when it comes, is low enough that only I can hear it.

"I owe you an apology," he says, and for a second I'm convinced I've fallen into an alternate dimension.

I blink at him, eyebrows shooting up. "Uh... for what? Breathing too sexily in my direction? Existing with cheekbones that should be illegal?"

He doesn't crack a smile. If anything, he looks even more serious — which is wildly unfair considering the heart palpitations he's currently causing.

"For the bond," he says, his voice soft but firm, the words landing with the weight of a guillotine.

I freeze, my mind tripping over itself. "Bond? What bond?"

Nyxian's eyes darken, his shadows stirring around him like smoke curling through the air. "It's already sealed," he says simply, like he's telling me the sky is blue or that water is wet.

I laugh. I *actually laugh*. It's a slightly deranged, coffee-deprived sound. "Uh, pretty sure I'd *remember* sealing a supernatural death contract, thanks."

His lips twitch — not a smile, more like the idea of one — and then he leans even closer, lowering his voice into that sinful, rumbly tone that makes my toes curl. "The night I entered your dream," he murmurs. "You asked for me. You accepted me. You let me in."

A beat.

"You sealed the bond when you begged for more."

I blink at him.

Once.

Twice.

Then a third time for good measure.

"You're telling me..." I start slowly, pointing a finger at him like he's a particularly confusing math problem, "that *dream sex* counts as legally binding in your world?"

"Yes," he says without hesitation.

I stare at him, mouth slightly open, brain running through all the questionable dream choices I've made in my life.

"And just to clarify," I say, holding up a hand like I'm cross-examining him, "this is because I—what—got a little handsy with the shadow tentacles and said, *oh yes, daddy more?*"

Nyxian's expression doesn't change, but his shadows shudder slightly around him — like they're just as affected by the memory as he is.

"You accepted me without fear. You wanted me. That is enough to forge the connection."

My jaw drops.

I lost my dignity and freedom in a dream because I was horny and emotionally vulnerable.

"*Oh my god,*" I groan, dropping my forehead dramatically onto the table with a loud *thunk*.

There's a low, rumbling sound from across the table. It takes me a second to realize Nyxian is *laughing*. A real, deep, chest-shaking laugh, like I just did something precious and stupid and he's drinking it in like fine wine.

I lift my head slowly, peering at him through my hair. "You owe me a *very fancy dinner* for this emotional damage."

"You already belong to me," he says, voice dipped in pure, lethal amusement. "I'll give you anything you want."

I squint at him, still recovering. "You say that now, but wait until you see my Amazon wishlist."

His smile — small, sharp, devastating — curves just enough to make my stomach somersault. "I already have."

Yeah.

I'm so screwed.

In *every* sense of the word.

Before I can even begin processing my new life choices, there's a loud, very obvious *gasp* from behind me.

I whip my head around to find Sadie leaning so far close to my face, peeking in with the worst "I'm not spying" face I have ever seen in my life. Song stands just behind her, looking mortified but doing a terrible job at hiding her own curiosity.

"*Girl.*" Sadie practically shrieks, slamming her body into her chair with zero shame. "You *dream-fucked* your way into supernatural marriage?!"

I groan and slap a hand over my face. "Can we *not* phrase it like that in front of the entire Court of Doom and Gloom?"

Sadie's eyes are the size of dinner plates. She spins toward the table, pointing dramatically at Nyxian. "And you—" she gasps, "—you didn't *even tell her* until now?!"

Nyxian doesn't even blink. "I didn't even fucking know it could happen."

Sadie throws up her hands. "Bro, *you gave her the full-rated R director's cut in her sleep* and now you wanna talk about *not knowing it could even fucking happen*?!"

I slam my forehead back on the table with another dramatic *thunk*.

Across from me, Nyxian's shadows are practically vibrating with restrained laughter. I swear the man is *enjoying this* way too much.

Vassago, who had been quietly sipping his coffee, sets his cup down with a slow, calculated smirk. "Well," he drawls, "at least she's efficient. Most mortals require complicated courting and bargaining... lot's of promises and persuasion. She just needed a good—"

"*Don't finish that sentence,*" I shout, lifting my head just enough to glare at him.

Sadie is cackling so hard now she's bent over at the waist, clutching her swollen stomach. Song fans her awkwardly from behind, whispering, "Maybe we should get her some water."

I lift a hand and weakly flip them all off without looking up.

Sadie, wiping tears from her eyes, plants herself right next to me at the table and pats my back dramatically. "Hey, Wynne. Honestly? You bagged yourself a ten. Dream seal or not, you could've done worse. You could've ended up with... I dunno, a soul-sucking demon or something."

I squint at her. "Sadie. Nyxian *is* a soul-sucking death reaper."

Sadie beams. "Yeah, but like, a *hot* one."

Nyxian, looking the definition of smug, leans back slightly in his chair, crossing his arms over his chest. His shadows practically purr at the compliment.

CHAPTER TWENTY-EIGHT

Nyxian

RIVER - BISHOP BRIGGS

I watch Wynne get dressed from across the room, my arms are folded, and my back is against the cold stone wall like I'm trying to merge with it. Her red hair sways with every small movement, catching the low light like a damn flame I can't extinguish.

I grit my teeth.

This is a fucking mess.

I had Ashton send one of his lackeys to grab her something more fitting for the Underworld—leather, dark fabrics, the sort of thing that doesn't scream *fresh blood, easy kill*. She looks ridiculous in it. Beautiful, sure, but still too soft, too *human* for this place.

I shift my weight, the growing tightness in my chest pissing me off more than I care to admit.

I'm still in denial.

Still clawing for some rational excuse that makes this feel like anything other than the betrayal it is.

Because that's what it feels like.

A betrayal of everything I was, everything I fought for.

A mortal mate.

Me.

It's fucking laughable.

Something that should've been nothing—some stupid dream, some moment of weakness twisted by her need and my...by the Gods, my fucking *stupidity*—turned into a blood-sealed bond. No persuasion, no begging. Just two broken creatures clawing for something they didn't even understand.

And now here I am. Shackled.

Bound to a woman who didn't even know what she was accepting.

Bound to a future I worry she never wanted.

I could rip the stars from the sky and it still wouldn't be enough to undo this.

She hums quietly under her breath, a soft, oblivious sound as she adjusts the belt around her waist. She doesn't know how dangerous this is. She doesn't realize what it means—to wear my mark in this place.

And yet...

The worst part?

It feels like a sin, yes.

But it also feels *right*.

And that?

That makes me want to tear the fucking world apart.

"You're staring," Wynne says without looking at me, her voice light, almost teasing.

I sneer before I can stop myself. "Maybe I'm just waiting to see if you trip over yourself. Wouldn't want my *mate* looking like a damn fool." The word tastes bitter in my mouth. A "demeaning term" in her own words.

She spins around, hands on her hips, fiery as ever. "Oh, please. You're just mad I look better in leather than you do."

My jaw tightens. Her mouth. Her *fucking mouth*. It's a wonder no one's killed her yet.

I stalk across the room, the shadows licking at my heels, and stop just shy of touching her. She tilts her chin up, unafraid, daring me.

I want to snarl.

I want to crush her mouth with mine and remind her exactly what she's dealing with.

Instead, I lean down, my voice a razor-sharp whisper against her ear. "Keep testing me, little disaster. See how long that mouth of yours lasts when I finally lose my patience and fuck some restraint into it."

She shivers, and for one glorious second, I think she finally understands the game she's playing.

But then she smirks—smirks, the stupid, beautiful, reckless idiot—and pats my chest like I'm some kind of pet.

"Down, boy," she says sweetly.

I almost laugh.

Almost.

Instead, I pull back, forcing the fire inside me to coil tighter, burning under my skin. I have to keep control. Have to remember who I am.

Because if I don't, if I give in to the chaos she brings out in me, I won't just lose my patience.

I'll lose myself.

And there won't be anything left of Nyxian but a shadow and a corpse.

Wynne reaches down and holds a firm grip on my growing bulge. We lock eyes. She smiles. "You owe me a few hours, you know?"

I don't move.

I don't breathe.

Her small hand, her stupid cocky smile — it lights a fire under my skin so hot it scalds the last threads of my control.

Every instinct screams at me to shove her against the wall, rip that smug look off her mouth with my teeth, and remind her that she's mine now.

Not just because she sealed the bond.

Not because fate said so.

Because I fucking *want* her to be.

"You're playing a dangerous game, little flame," I say, my voice dark and low enough to make her eyes dilate. "And you're not ready for how it ends."

Her fingers tighten slightly — not enough to hurt, but enough to make sure I feel it.

As if I could ever not feel her.

"I think I can handle it," she says, all sugar and spite, like she's daring me to break her.

By Gods, I should hate her.

I should resent her for putting me in this situation and forcing me into falling for her.

Instead, I want to drag her down into the depths with me and never let her surface again.

I grab her wrist — not hard enough to hurt, but enough to remind her who's stronger — and slowly peel her hand off me.

I curl my fingers around her delicate wrist, feeling her pulse hammering under her skin, and something savage and soft stirs in my chest.

I hate it.

I fucking *crave* it.

"You think you're so clever," I mutter, tugging her closer until she's pressed against me, until there's no space between us but air and rage and the sick, sweet gravity of what we are.

Her breath stutters.

Not in fear.

No, not in fear.

She's *reckless* enough to *like* it.

"And you think you're *so* scary," she says breathlessly, glaring up at me with all the fury of a star about to go supernova.

I grin then — a real one, vicious and brutal.

I dip my head, brushing my mouth over her jaw, her ear, not kissing, just letting her feel the threat in the promise.

"I don't think, little flame," I whisper. "I *know*."

She shivers — glorious, unguarded.

And despite everything—despite the voice in my head screaming that she doesn't belong here, that she's a mistake—I find myself *softening*, just a fraction.

Only for her.

"Get undressed," I say, releasing her and stepping back, shoving every fucked-up, raging instinct deep into the black pit of my being where it belongs.

She looks up at me with those big blue eyes—sensual, perfect.

In all her imperfection, she *is* fucking perfect.

She worked so hard to get this outfit on. To blend in. To fit into my fucked-up little world.

And now, she slowly unbuckles the belt she just fought to secure.

She doesn't break eye contact. Instead, she sends me a sly, knowing smile—like she's fully aware of what she's doing.

Holding the belt out by two fingers, she clicks her tongue as it drops. "Boom," she whispers.

She's testing me. Testing how far she can push, how much restraint I really have.

I raise an eyebrow, pulse ticking in my throat.

She's teasing, glistening with a sheen of sweat—turned on. She's wild and electric.

She starts to unbutton her shirt, slow and deliberate, peeling it from her shoulders to reveal freckles I wish I could kiss away.

God, I want to take them from her. Take all of it.

But that's not something I can erase. Not a past I can rewrite.

183

And fuck, I hate that.

I hate that I can't carry some of her pain for her.

Her shirt hits the floor. Neon pink bra.

I tilt my head, because I know how it must burn that she can't wear her favorite color here.

She has to hide it.

Has to change herself just to survive in this place.

I hate that too.

But if she doesn't blend in, she becomes a target.

And I can't fight the world to protect her.

Can't exile everyone.

Can't kill them all.

She turns around, fumbling with the button of her pants.

She hooks her fingers into the waistband and peels them down... revealing a neon pink G-string.

Her ass—full, perfect.

Freckles trail down her spine, dotting the curve of her hips, down to her thighs.

A heat ignites in me. Hatred. Possession.

She's *mine*.

She's *fucking* mine, and I'll kill *anyone* who *thinks* they can touch her again.

I reach out, take her hand, and spin her toward me.

Our mouths crash together in a kiss that robs her breath—and mine.

One hand tangled in her fiery hair.

The other gripping her ass, pulling her flush against me.

She squeals into my mouth, and I swallow it whole.

Her body melts into mine like she was fucking *made* for me.

Like the gods carved her from my rib and stitched her together with fire and silk.

She grips my shoulders, nails biting through the fabric of my shirt, but I don't stop. I *can't* stop.

Not when she looks at me like that.

Like I'm not a monster. Like I am *just* Nyxian... Like I'm *hers*.

My mouth trails down her neck, teeth scraping against that spot that makes her tremble.

She gasps—and it's not fear. It's need. It's trust.

And it's dangerous.

I press her back until she hits the wall, and she lets me cage her there like a willing little flame, flickering and wild. I kiss her jaw, her throat, my tongue dragging across her skin as my hand slides under the thin strap of that ridiculous pink bra.

"Wynne," I growl against her skin, "You keep testing me like that, and I *will* break every rule I've ever made for you."

She tilts her head back and whispers, "Then break them."

Fuck.

My restraint cracks like ice beneath a wildfire.

I grab her thighs and lift her effortlessly, pinning her against the wall. She wraps her legs around me, and her breath fans against my ear.

"Tell me," She murmurs, "Tell me I'm yours."

I press my forehead to hers; eyes locked on those sea-glass blues. "My name is carved into your bones, little flame," I whisper. "You've always been mine. And by gods help the bastard who tries to take you from me."

She shudders, her lips parting. "Then *prove* it."

My control dies.

I slam my mouth back onto hers, one hand bracing the wall, the other sliding up her spine to the clasp of her bra. I tear it open like it offended me, like it ever had the right to touch her skin.

She gasps, but she doesn't stop me.

Her nails scratch down my chest as I pull back just enough to look at her—*really* look.

Flushed, panting, trembling with need... and still defiant.

Still *herself*.

"You make me crazy," I admit, voice rough. "You are chaos wrapped in skin, and I fucking love it."

She smirks. "Good. Because I'm not stopping."

Neither am I.

Her smirk lights a fuse in my blood.

"I'm not stopping," she says again, softer this time, but with that same challenge in her voice.

I don't answer with words.

I press her harder into the wall, grind my hips against her, and she moans—a high, breathless sound that makes my vision go black around the edges. She can feel how hard I am for her. How fucking ready I am to be inside of her again.

I grip the back of her neck, tilt her face up, and kiss her again—deeper this time, bruising and filthy. My tongue claims her like she's air and I've been suffocating without her. Her thighs tighten around me, pulling me closer, rolling her hips into me until I'm barely holding on.

She breaks the kiss with a gasp. "The bed—"

"No." My voice is gravel. "Right here."

Right where I lost my mind for her. Right where she undressed like a fucking siren and dared me to lose control.

I drag her g-string down her thighs, letting it fall to the floor like silk. She's bare for me now—glistening, shaking, so fucking perfect. I run my fingers through her folds, teasing, letting her feel how slow I can make it before I *ruin* her.

She bucks into my hand, and I chuckle darkly. "So eager."

"You're the one who told me to get undressed," she pants, lips parted and eyes wild.

"I didn't say I'd be gentle."

I slide two fingers into her, curling them just right, and she gasps again—hands fisting in my shirt, legs trembling around my waist. She's soaked. Hot and tight and dripping for me.

I fuck her with my fingers while watching every twitch of her expression—how she bites her lip, how her lashes flutter, how her breath catches right before she breaks.

"You like being against the wall?" I murmur against her throat, licking a line up to her ear. "Being held like this, spread open for me?"

She nods, frantic. "Yes—fuck, *yes*, Nyxian—"

I drop my belt and shove my pants down just enough to free my swollen cock. I'm already leaking, aching, pulsing with the need to be inside her. My tip drags through her slick folds, and we both hiss at the contact.

One thrust, and I'm buried in her to the hilt.

Her head hits the wall. Her nails dig into my shoulders. Her mouth falls open in a silent scream.

"Fuck," I groan. "You feel like sin."

She tightens around me, her walls fluttering like she's already close. She's always been so responsive for me, so *good* for me, even when she's being a goddamn menace.

I pull out and slam back in. Hard. Fast. Deep.

Her cry echoes in the room.

I piston into her. My pace is brutal and unrelenting. The slap of our bodies, the wet sounds, the gasps and curses—it's all too much, but also not enough. She kisses me like she's starving and moans like she wants the whole world to hear.

I reach between us, rub tight circles against her clit, and she shatters in my arms.

Her pussy clenches around me like a vice, and I lose it.

With a growl ripped from my chest, I bury myself deep one last time and come hard—hot and fast, teeth clenched, forehead pressed to hers as we fall apart together.

We stay like that for a second. Breathing each other in. Our sweat mixing. Our bodies still tangled and twitching with the aftermath.

She brushes her lips over mine. "You gonna help me find my underwear?"

I smirk. "Fuck your underwear."

CHAPTER TWENTY-NINE

Wynne

EARNED IT - THE WEEKND

My back is still pressed to the wall, my legs trembling, my heart thundering like a war drum against my ribs.

Nyxian hasn't moved. He's still inside me. Still holding me like he owns me.

And maybe... maybe he does.

I blink, trying to catch my breath, my lips still tingling from how hard he kissed me. Took me. Claimed me like I belonged to him the moment I walked through the gates of his world.

Fuck, I should be scared.

But I'm not.

I'm wrecked. Flushed. Dripping in sweat and slick and something I don't have the words for yet.

His hand is still in my hair, his other on my hip like he's trying to fuse me to him. Like if he lets go, I'll vanish.

"I can't think when you look at me like that," I whisper.

"Then stop thinking," he murmurs, voice rough, lips grazing my temple. "Just feel."

I do.

I feel everything. The ache between my thighs. The way his chest still rises hard and fast against mine. The faint tremble in his arm like he lost control, and hated how much he loved it.

This wasn't just fucking.

It wasn't even just claiming.

It was war.

And I'm not sure if I lost or won.

I run my fingers through his sweat-damp hair and let my head fall back against the wall, eyes closing. "You said you wouldn't be gentle."

"I'm never gentle." His voice has that dangerous edge again, but it's quieter now. Almost soft. Almost guilty.

But when I open my eyes and meet his gaze, I don't see guilt.

I see obsession.

Possession.

Something far darker than love.

And somehow, I want it. I want *him.*

"You're insane," I breathe, smiling a little even as my body hums like a live wire.

He finally pulls out of me, and I wince at the loss, his hands steadying me as I slide down from the wall. My legs barely hold me, and I laugh, shaky and high.

He catches me.

Of course he does...

Nyxian lowers me gently onto the couch, then kneels in front of me, his large hands resting on my thighs. His thumb draws soft circles on my skin as if he's trying to soothe the storm he just unleashed.

"You're mine now," he says it like a vow. A warning. A fucking prophecy.

I tilt my head. "You said that before."

"I meant it then." His eyes lock on mine. "But now? Now I *feel* it. In every bone, every breath. You belong to me."

And despite every red flag, every bit of fire in his eyes, every warning bell screaming in my head—

I want to believe him.

I want to see where this madness leads.

Even if it *burns me alive*.

Nyxian doesn't move for a long moment. He's still crouched in front of me, breathing hard, eyes wild like some beast that hasn't quite come down from the hunt.

And me?

I'm wrecked. Ruined. Ravished. My thighs are trembling, my chest rising and falling like I just ran ten miles in heels.

But I'm still me.

And that means I can't just sit in silence like some lovesick little lamb.

So I blink down at him and deadpan, "Well. That was... violent?"

His head lifts slowly. His mouth twitches. "You didn't seem to mind."

"Oh, I minded." I lift a finger dramatically. "But only because I'm going to walk like a baby deer on a frozen pond for the next week."

He grunts, amused, rubbing a palm down his face.

"I'm serious," I go on, lifting a brow as I try to shift and wince at the ache between my legs. "You rearranged some very important organs. I think one of my ovaries is in my throat."

He chuckles this time—a real, rough, deep sound that rolls from his chest like thunder.

Fuck. *That* sound.

I glance down and tug the hem of the shirt he threw at me earlier, trying to cover myself at least a little. His eyes track the movement like a predator.

"Don't start," I warn, holding up a hand. "You already tried to break me in half. I need, like, electrolytes and a juice box before I even think about round two."

Nyxian moves closer, kneeling again so he's between my legs. His hands slide up my thighs, but this time... it's gentler. Slower. Like he's taking in what he did. What *we* did.

"You're beautiful when you're wrecked," he says.

I snort. "I bet you say that to all the women you rail against a wall."

"I don't," he says simply, and that sincerity—raw and sudden—makes me go quiet.

I look at him for a beat, then mutter, "Well, shit. Now I feel something. This is terrible."

He smirks, clearly enjoying himself now.

"You're insufferable," I grumble, even as I let him press a kiss to my knee.

"You love it."

"I didn't *say* that."

"But you're still here," he says, and there's something dangerous and knowing in his voice.

And he's right.

I *am* still here.

Even when I shouldn't be. Even when every logical part of me is screaming *danger*.

I look at him, really look at him—and despite all the fire, the obsession, the madness...

I feel *safe*.

And that? That's the scariest part of all.

And he doesn't even say much about the accidental bond—this "dark claim" they're calling it. It's like the universe decided to tie us together with no warning, no explanation. No real *fucking* consent.

But of course, I'm not complaining. Oh no. That would require me to admit I don't want this. And I do. God damn, help me... Because I fucking *do*.

I should run for the fucking hills, I should try to escape this predicament my horny ass self found myself in, but—

I look at him. The way his dark eyes burn into me. The way his jaw tightens every time I move or breathe.

The way he's so fucking sure of this.

I'm stuck, aren't I?

But somehow, I'm comfortable. I'm happy. I feel fucking safe.

And it doesn't make sense. None at all. But I lean into him anyway, every part of me betraying my better judgment.

Fuck it. I could run. I could leave. I could go back to my life—my real life.

But when he pulls me closer, his arms around me like a vice, my stupid, traitorous heart just says: *No. Stay.*

I should've expected this kind of chaos. Hell, I was practically asking for it. But I don't feel like a victim. Not here. Not with him.

"Wynne?" His voice is rough, like the whole night has shredded him too.

I meet his gaze, keeping that defiant smile in place, even though there's a strange heat in my chest. "What?"

"Are you scared of me still?" he asks, eyes darker than ever, voice low, searching.

I tilt my head, considering it. Then I grin. "If I'm being honest? No. But you are starting to give off some serious 'I'm going to ruin your life in the worst possible way' vibes."

He laughs, the sound harsh and strained. "I've never claimed to be a good male."

"Clearly." I stretch a little, feeling the ache between my legs again. "But that's part of your charm."

He growls, a low, warning sound. "Careful."

"Why? You going to punish me?" I roll my eyes, teasing. "Because if I didn't know any better, I'd think this whole bond thing is your way of marking your territory."

His expression darkens again, but this time, there's something softer underneath the storm—something raw.

And that?

That makes me *nervous*.

"So what is my role here?" I ask him, arms crossed loosely over my chest, trying to sound casual, like I'm not freaked the fuck out by this whole mess we've gotten ourselves into. "Now that I'm a part of this world?"

He shifts slightly, the hint of a smirk tugging at his lips as he looks down at me. "I'm taking over Exu's position. Azrael is having our home built now for us."

I raise an eyebrow, processing that. "Oh." I nod slowly. "So I will be like a bored housewife, huh? With nothing to do but look pretty, keep the house clean, and maybe plan dinner parties for all your high-society psychopaths?"

His lips twitch, but he doesn't laugh. "If you want to call it that, sure. But we will have help."

I snort, shaking my head. "Oh, great. So, I'll have a staff of *highly-trained psychopaths* to make sure the place doesn't burn down while I'm playing housewife?" I raise an eyebrow, trying to keep the humor in my tone, even though the whole thing feels surreal. "What's next? A personal army to guard the mansion while I do yoga and drink overpriced coffee?"

His lips quirk in that way that makes my insides do that annoying fluttering thing. "Something like that. But I'll keep you occupied." His gaze darkens as his eyes flick over me in a way that makes my pulse quicken. "Trust me, you won't have time to be bored."

I let out a breath, trying to tamp down the heat his words stir inside me. "Oh? And what exactly am I supposed to do while I'm not busy with my 'bored housewife' duties?"

His gaze lingers for a beat longer than necessary, before he shrugs slightly, as if toying with the idea. "Whatever I want you to do."

I tilt my head, crossing my arms more firmly over my chest. "Oh, really? Sounds like you've already planned out my whole life for me."

He steps forward, a predatory glint in his eyes. "I haven't even scratched the surface yet."

A small thrill runs through me, despite myself. I should be angry, should be fighting this idea of being confined to whatever role he's envisioning for me. But there's a part of me that wants this life he has planned for me.

"Well," I finally say, voice laced with mock sweetness. "I guess I'll just have to keep you entertained then, huh? Might be hard for a *busy man* like you."

He pauses, his smirk turning into something darker, more dangerous. "You're already doing a damn good job of that, Wynne."

A little shiver runs down my spine at the way he says my name, and for a second, I wonder what the hell I've gotten myself into. But when I look at him—really look at him—I realize I'm not sure I care anymore.

"Excuse me, sir, but I believe my new name is *Little Disaster*." I raise an eyebrow, feigning an air of importance, even though I know I'm about to burst into laughter at the ridiculousness of it.

He smirks, not missing a beat. "I dunno. *Wynne* has a ring to it."

I wince, the sharp edge of his casual use of my name sending a wave of unwanted heat through me. It isn't like I've *grown* accustomed to his fucked-up pet names for me or anything. Nope. Totally *not* a thing.

I roll my eyes. "Oh, so now you're just going to pretend we're all normal, huh? Just Wynne? No *Little Disaster*, no *Ember of Life*, just—what— *Wynne*?"

His lips curve in that knowing, amused way. "Wynne has a nice sound to it. And I'm not into over-complicating things."

I sneer, my sarcasm flowing as naturally as breathing. "I liked *Ember of Life* better, fucker."

He offers a light chuckle. "We need to be in the dining room. We have a lot to discuss with the group about the upcoming events."

I roll my eyes, pushing myself off the wall and following him. "Of course. 'A lot to discuss,' just a casual meeting where we all pretend to be normal." I mutter, the sarcasm heavy in my voice. "How exciting."

He doesn't bite, just glancing over his shoulder with that knowing smirk still playing on his lips. "Trust me, if you think this is boring, you won't like the next few days."

"Great," I respond, my voice dripping with mock enthusiasm. "Can't wait. I live for this *thrilling* existence."

As we walk down the hallway, I can't help but wonder just how much more 'excitement' I'm going to be dragged into. A part of me wants to run, to escape this strange mess I've found myself in, but I can't seem to make my legs move faster than his pace. It's like I'm trapped in this vortex of tension and attraction, and the only way out is deeper in.

"Do I get to know what the *'group'* is discussing, or is that a 'secret club' kind of thing?" I ask, trying to keep my tone light, even though I'm genuinely curious.

He glances back at me, the faintest glimmer of something more intense flickering in his eyes. "I'll fill you in when we get there. But you might want to *really* listen. There's more going on than you realize."

I raise an eyebrow, more interested now than before. "More going on? You mean other than my incredible ability to fuck things up in record time?"

CHAPTER THIRTY

Nyxian

ARSONIST'S LULABYE - HOZIER

"Are you sure this is what you really want to do?" Azrael asks Exu, voice rough like gravel, blonde mortal hair sticking up in chaotic tufts—like he just got done fucking Layla into a mattress and barely remembered to show up to this damn meeting.

I glance at her. Collected. Too calm. The kind of calm people wear like armor when they're praying no one sees the panic slipping through the cracks. She's scared. Not much—but enough for me to notice. Enough to make me wonder what the hell this meeting is *really* about.

Exu stands near the edge of the courtyard, skin slick with sweat from wrapping up what'll be his last training session—his last time standing in this role. My role now. The weight of it tastes bitter in my mouth. All of this—the planning, the false smiles, the exchanging of responsibilities—is to topple one male.

Hades.

Our so-called "father". The Lord of the Underworld. A walking fucking disappointment wrapped in arrogance and soaked in blood.

"I think I've spent enough time under Hades' thumb," Exu says, eyes tired but firm. "I don't want to be around for the next time he calls on me like I'm some glorified lapdog. I'd rather be in the mortal realm. Help Luca with the café."

I arch a brow at that. A *café*. What a downgrade.

My gaze slides to Luca. The smell hits first—wet dog and forest musk. He reeks of wolf, and yet no one here even flinches. Not a wrinkle of the nose. Not a twitch. They pretend like it doesn't offend every supernatural instinct we were born with.

He keeps his head down, staring at his hands like some guilt-stricken idiot. But I know better. He plays docile, plays innocent, but underneath? He's a predator. Like the rest of us. He just has the luxury of pretending he isn't.

"I hate that you ended up going to Saygin after all, Luca," Azrael says with a sigh. "Layla and I told you we would help you rebuild."

"I wanted an exact replica of what I lost," Luca replies, offering one of those half-assed smiles he thinks makes him likable. "Before you lot came into my life."

He makes it sound like *we're* the problem. Maybe he's not entirely wrong.

Sadie slaps him on the back with more affection than I think he deserves. "You're gonna miss us. Don't act like you aren't, pretty boy."

She's so round now she looks like she could pop at any second. Swollen with life. A strange thing, seeing her like this—loud, glowing, unbothered by the war the rest of us are dragging into existence. Carrying Ashton's heir like it's just another day.

Wynne sits beside me, uncharacteristically quiet. Observing. Absorbing. Her confusion pulses off her like waves of heat, but she's smart enough not to interrupt. I don't say anything to her—not yet—but I feel her gaze flick to me more than once, like she's trying to read a language she hasn't learned yet.

Ashton leans back in his chair, too relaxed, too calm. "There's a disturbance in Olde Towne. We need to head out soon."

Azrael tenses. "What kind of disturbance?"

"Beings who are loyal to Hades," Ashton says. "They've caught wind of the revolt. They're hunting down anyone they suspect of joining our cause. Killing them in the streets. Executing anyone young or vulnerable. We've lost more this week than in the last few years combined." His voice drops lower. "Birth rates have tanked. Every young one lost is a blow we can't afford. If we keep bleeding out like this, we'll never rebuild an army strong enough to challenge Hades. No fresh blood means no future. No retirement. Just an endless loop of war."

He glances toward Sadie as if explaining to her more than the rest of us.

She frowns. "Will our son be in the army?"

Ashton nods, brushing her wild, curly black hair back with a gentleness that makes me nauseous. "When he's of age, he'll take my place."

Orcus hisses from his perch. "That is not a cue to start pumping out more Sadie spawns. One's enough."

Sadie flips him off with a grin. Orcus seems pleased by the reaction by the glow he gives in response.

I shift forward, ignoring the idiot Scythe and the domestic bullshit around me. "What about my house?" I ask Azrael directly. I'm done with pleasantries of war.

Azrael glances at Wynne before answering, and that alone pisses me off.

"We're nearly finished. You two just need to attend the auction to hire help. Maids. Security. Whatever else she wants. I already arranged an interior designer to meet with her soon so she can decorate it the way she wants—per your request."

I narrow my eyes at Wynne. "No pink."

She pouts.

Of fucking course she does.

She pouts, and I swear to every god in this cursed realm, if she bats her lashes at me again like that shit actually works on me— No.

Not right now.

I grip the edge of the table, jaw tight. "Don't even think about it."

Her pout deepens. "Fine. No pink." She tilts her head, eyes sparkling with mischief. "Maybe coral?"

Azrael chokes on his drink. Layla bites back a laugh. Even Ashton smirks.

I stare, flat and unblinking. "Wynne."

"I'm just saying—it's like pink with a tan. Very regal. Very... revenge-core."

Sadie snorts. "She's got you on the ropes already."

I roll my shoulders, cracking the tension in my spine. "I'm not on the ropes. I'm building the ropes she'll hang herself with if she tries to sneak blush tones into my war room."

Wynne kicks me under the table. Hard enough to be noticed. Light enough not to be a challenge. "Noted. We'll go with blood red and soul black, just for you, *dear.*"

"Right, Little Disaster."

She doesn't smile—not right away. But her eyes burn. That same fire that got her into this mess. That same fire that *keeps* her here.

And for one brief, quiet moment, I forget that there's a war clawing at our gates.

Ashton's voice cuts through the last thread of amusement. "We need to move. Now."

The shift in the room is immediate. Gone is the teasing. The laughter. The pretending that everything isn't bleeding at the seams.

Azrael straightens, the easy calm replaced with something colder—calculated. "Exu, you'll take point on organizing who's staying behind."

Exu nods once, already in motion.

"We'll handle the sweep in Olde Towne," Azrael continues. "Anyone we find loyal to Hades, anyone still killing innocents—we show no mercy. No trials. No exile. Just ash."

There's something vicious in the way he says it. I like that version of him better. Less crown-polishing, more throat-ripping.

I rise to my feet, every joint tight, ready. My hands itch for violence—for the sharp, familiar taste of vengeance split open across my knuckles. It's been too quiet. Too many meetings. Too much pretending that strategy is stronger than fear. Too many delicate dances with diplomacy while the world burns.

I need something to break. I need blood.

Then—

Wynne grabs my arm.

I stop mid-step. Look down at her hand, her delicate fingers curled around my wrist like she's tethering me. Like she *thinks* she can hold me here.

Her voice is small. But not weak. Never weak.

"Please," she says. "Stay."

That word. It hits somewhere it shouldn't. Lodges deep like a dagger made of guilt and need.

I glance toward the others—Azrael, Ashton, Vassago—already moving away, discussing formation and sweep routes like I'm not part of this war too. Like I'm something else entirely.

Which I am.

And they *know* it.

They don't ask me to join them.

They know I don't play nice with leashes.

And yet...

I look down at Wynne again. Her brows are drawn tight, her eyes wide but steady. She's not afraid *of* me—she's afraid *for* me.

It's stupid.

I don't need her protection.

But gods, I want to stay.

I want to give her something she can hold onto.

I *hate* that I want that.

"My Ember of Life," I mutter, low enough it's just between us, "this is war. You think this ends with hand-holding and happy endings?"

She shakes her head once. "No. But I'm asking you to stay with me anyway."

Something claws at my ribs from the inside. A feral thing that wants to love her and ruin her in the same breath.

I'm not used to being needed.

I'm used to being *feared*.

And she doesn't flinch when I look at her like this—when every part of me is straining not to shred the world apart with my bare hands.

I brush her hand off gently. Not coldly. Not cruelly. Just enough to make her lift her eyes to mine.

"I'll come back," I say, and I fucking mean it.

Because now there's something worth coming back to.

CHAPTER THIRTY-ONE

Wynne

CONTROL - ZOE WEES

H ere I am.

Fucking stuck in the Underworld version of a girls' night with a bunch of women I barely know.

Do we catfight? Gossip?

Pluck each other's eyebrows while talking about the men who nearly got themselves killed for sport?

I have no idea what's expected of me here.

No one handed me a pamphlet on "how to be the warlord's maybe-girlfriend and survive an awkward tea party with the Queen of Death and her merry band of chaos wives."

We're all just sitting in the living room like it's normal.

Sadie is stretched across the couch like a tired goddess, one arm draped dramatically over her swollen belly, the other holding a juice pouch she definitely bullied Ashton into getting her.

Layla is curled in an oversized chair, legs tucked beneath her, flipping through some thick book that looks ancient. A soft glow pulses from the pages—magic or murder, probably both. Her sickle, I think she said his name is Drepane—yes, she just *has it casually lying around*—rests against the chair, the edge gleaming like it's bored and wants to cut something.

And then there's the cat.

"Flo."

Except calling her a cat is like calling a hurricane a breeze.

The tiger-beast is sprawled across the hearth like she owns the place. Which, judging by the way she keeps side-eyeing me like I'm a snack she hasn't decided whether to eat or not, she probably *does*.

I sit perched on the arm of a chair, one leg bouncing, because I can't settle.

Because everything feels off.

Because Nyxian left, and now I'm here with strangers wearing the faces of queens.

And I am... what?

A redhead with attitude. A survivor. A pawn with teeth.

Layla glances up from her book, her storm-colored eyes sharp. "You're making the UnderCat nervous."

"I'm making *her* nervous?" I scoff. "She's the size of a truck and purring like a chainsaw."

Flo lifts her head slightly. That is not a purr. That's a *warning*.

"She can sense how nervous you are and that is unsettling to her." Layla doesn't even look up from her book, still absorbed in whatever ancient chaos is written on the pages.

I glance at Flo again.

She's watching me like she's already calculated how many bites it would take to eat me whole.

I shift in my seat, leg still bouncing like a warning drum under my skin. I hate feeling like this—out of place, out of control. Like I'm in someone else's house wearing clothes that don't fit, pretending I belong.

"I'm not nervous," I lie.

Sadie hums knowingly, eyes still closed. "Sure, and I'm not bloated and cranky with a baby who kicks me in the bladder every five minutes."

Layla turns a page delicately. "She's not judging you, Wynne. She's just... watching."

"That's so much worse," I mutter.

"She does it to everyone at first," Layla says. "She tried to eat Azrael once."

Sadie snorts. "Azrael deserved it."

There's a pause. Then we all laugh, even me, though mine feels like a rusty door creaking open.

It's strange, this moment. Not quite friendship. Not quite peace. But something close enough to touch if I let myself reach for it.

But I don't.

Instead, I glance at Drepane—the sickle, her weapon, whatever the hell he is—and for a second, I swear the blade *shifts*. Just a flicker, a shimmer along the edge like it's paying attention too.

Nope.

Nope, nope, nope.

"I need air," I say, pushing to my feet.

Sadie cracks one eye open. "You're in the Underworld, babe. Good luck with that."

"I don't know *how* to relax!" I snap, voice cracking as the words tumble out.

It's not graceful. It's not dramatic. It's just *honest*. And it stings more than I expected.

Sadie lifts her head from the couch, her hair a wild halo around her face. "Ugh. Just talk. Stop overthinking."

"Talk about *what*?" My throat is tight. I can feel the burn behind my eyes. It's too much. It's all just too much. "I'm not crying because I'm sad, okay? I'm overwhelmed, and my face is leaking like a faulty faucet."

Sadie doesn't flinch. Doesn't judge. Just... shrugs.

"Well, how's sex with Shadow Daddy?"

That derails everything.

I blink. "I—what?"

She grins like a devil in designer boots. "You heard me. You're clearly stressed. Let's bond over dicks. I'll tell you what it's like with the Sandman if you spill about Sir Tall-Dark-and-Broody. Layla never talks about her sex life and it's *rude*. I deserve to live vicariously through you two."

"Shadow Daddy?" I repeat, incredulous.

Layla makes a sound suspiciously like a snort behind her book but says nothing.

Sadie waves a hand. "You're telling me Nyxian doesn't give *major* dominant energy? Come on. That male growls like he's got a PhD in ruin-you-without-trying."

"Wynne is literally having a panic attack," Layla says mildly, eyes still scanning her pages. "Maybe wait five minutes before diving into kinks?"

"She didn't know what to talk about, I offered a topic." Sadie shrugs. "You want a juice pouch?"

I wipe angrily at my face, the tears still falling even as I half-laugh, half-sob. "I don't know if I want to laugh or scream."

"Do both," Sadie says, sitting up and patting the couch. "Welcome to womanhood in the Underworld."

I hesitate. For a full ten seconds, I actually *consider* walking over and curling up next to Sadie like we're lifelong besties in a high school sleepover movie.

Then Flo shifts by the fireplace, lets out a low growl-purr hybrid, and I sit my ass *right back down*.

"No offense, but I feel like if I move too fast, your hell-beast will eat me."

"She likes you," Sadie says, sipping her juice like this is all perfectly normal. "If she wanted to eat you, she'd already be chewing."

Comforting.

I glance at Layla, who still hasn't looked up from her glowing murder-book. "You're just going to sit there and not stop her?"

"She's not dangerous unless you're a threat." Layla flips a page. "Or bleeding. Or anxious."

"Cool. Good to know. I'll just hold in my entire personality."

Sadie laughs, and it's this bright, sharp thing—like a chime made of chaos. "You really don't know how to do this, huh?"

"Do what?"

"Girl time. Sitting still. Existing with other women without assuming it's a trap."

I open my mouth to argue, but... she's not wrong.

My whole life has been one long, jagged game of survival. Women were competition. Enemies. Rumormongers with sharp nails and sharper smiles. Pretty packages hiding poison.

So now I'm here, surrounded by literal royalty and a demi-goddess with a tiger for a pet, and I feel like a feral alley cat dumped at a tea party.

"I'm not used to this," I mumble. "Any of this."

Sadie's expression softens. "None of us were. Not really. You think I came out the womb bonded to the damn Sandman? Layla used to be a total disaster too. And I mean that *lovingly*."

"Thanks," Layla mutters, still not looking up.

"I'm not saying trust us overnight," Sadie adds. "But you could start by trusting that we don't want to eat you."

"Speak for yourself," Flo mutters.

I jump. "*She talks?*"

Layla finally closes her book. "Only when she feels like being extra."

Sadie winks. "You'll get used to it."

I blink at the tiger-beast, who yawns like I'm not worth the calories.

Right. Totally normal girls' night.

Then Sadie pats the couch again. "Now. Tell me if Shadow Daddy bites or not."

I sigh, dragging my hands down my face.

"He doesn't *bite*," I mutter. "He *consumes*. Like I'm something he's waited for centuries to have."

Layla looks up. Sadie's jaw drops.

"Well, damn," Sadie breathes. "*That's* a line."

"I blacked out during most of it," I admit. "I think he did too. There were shadows. Restraints. My spine still hurts, but I also haven't stopped smiling in three days, so."

Layla blinks. "I take it back. You're *not* a disaster. You're one of us."

Flo purrs again.

And this time, it actually sounds like approval.

"I mean... I didn't *mean* for it to happen like that," I continue, fiddling with a loose thread on the chair cushion. "The first time, I think he was trying to prove he owns me or something."

Layla tilts her head. "That tracks."

"He's insufferable," I say. "Bossy. Controlling. Has this way of looming like he owns the air in the room."

"But?" Sadie says, already grinning.

"But he *sees* me," I whisper, and just like that, the sarcasm slips. "Not just the attitude. Not just the red hair and the rage and the stubborn streak. He sees the ugly. The broken. And he doesn't flinch."

Layla's smile is faint but genuine. "That's rare."

"I didn't think anyone ever would," I admit. "I've always been *too much* or *not enough*. Too angry, too loud, too damaged. But with him... fuck, with him I feel *safe*. Which is insane, because he's literally a reaper with blood-stained hands and a history of violence."

"You like the blood," Sadie says. "Admit it."

"I *do* like the blood," I groan. "I like the possessiveness. The way he says *'mine'* like it's not up for debate. The way he looks at me like I'm the only damn thing anchoring him to sanity."

Layla leans forward slightly. "He needs that. Something real. Something *tethering*."

I nod. "And I need someone who doesn't back away when I bare my teeth."

There's a pause. A gentle silence. Like the room is holding its breath.

Then Sadie laughs. "Okay, but have you told him that?"

I blink. "Told him *what*?"

"That you're in love with him."

"I—" I start. Then stop. "I didn't say that."

"Oh honey," Sadie says, grinning wide. "You didn't have to."

"I'm not *in love*," I say, instantly on the defensive. "I'm just... obsessed. Emotionally compromised. Deeply attracted. Maybe slightly enchanted."

"You sound like Layla when she was in denial," Sadie teases.

"I was *not* in denial," Layla protests. "I was... resisting fate."

"Denial," Sadie and I say at the same time.

I exhale, letting my head fall back against the chair. "Fine. Maybe I'm falling. Just a little. Like... terminal velocity with no parachute. But I'm not ready to say it out loud."

"You just did," Layla says, smirking.

Flo snorts from the hearth like she's heard this whole song and dance a hundred times before.

I let the moment sit, warm and weird and unexpectedly safe. Maybe girl time isn't all bad.

"Next time," Sadie says, stretching. "You're bringing snacks. That's the price of emotional vulnerability."

"I'll bring cookies," I mutter.

"And that's why you're one of us," Layla says, curling back into her chair.

And for the first time since Nyxian walked away, I don't feel completely alone.

Sadie's playful smile drops like a rock.

She shifts on the couch, eyes narrowing as she turns toward Layla. "Hey... do you feel that?"

Layla slowly lifts her head from her book, gaze distant like she's listening to something I can't hear. "Yeah," she says after a beat. "Something's... wrong."

Wrong.

The word slams into me like a knife between the ribs, and I don't know why. I sit up straighter, cold creeping into my limbs.

"What do you mean, *wrong*?" I ask, voice brittle, brittle like glass about to shatter. "What are you feeling?"

Sadie rubs a hand over her belly. "Something tight. Like panic... or pain. It's not mine. Ashton's feeling it, which means I'm feeling it."

I blink. "Wait, what? You can feel his emotions?"

They both glance at each other, like I just asked if fire is hot.

Layla leans forward, tone gentler now. "You don't know?"

"Know what?"

"It's part of the bond," Sadie says. "Once it's formed, you and your mate can feel each other's emotions. Sometimes even communicate telepathically—usually if the bond's really deep."

My mouth goes dry. "But... I'm not bonded." I say it, but even I don't believe it. Not fully. No matter how many times Nyxian tried to explain that we are "bonded".

Layla tilts her head. "Aren't you?"

And I freeze.

Because that *wrong* feeling... that twisting knot in my stomach that won't let me breathe, that sharp edge behind my ribs like something inside me is bracing for impact—

It *isn't mine.*

It's his.

Nyxian.

That heavy, angry, storming feeling... the one I've been ignoring for the last few minutes, trying to pretend it was just nerves—it's not mine.

It's him.

I jump to my feet. "Something's happened."

Sadie sits up too, her juice pouch falling to the floor unnoticed. "You *are* bonded."

"I didn't know," I breathe. "I didn't—I thought it was just the way he talked—"

Layla closes her book with a snap. "It doesn't matter. If you feel it, it's real. Try reaching for him. In your mind. Like... thinking, but *louder*. Direct it at him. Picture his face. Call him."

"I don't know how!"

"You don't need to *know*," Layla says. "Just feel."

So I do.

I close my eyes, heart hammering, and I let the panic rise, let it crawl up my throat and turn into something wild.

I picture him—Nyxian—his scowl, the way he looks at me like I'm both a problem and a prize. His ridiculous black hair. That terrible mouth.

I reach for him in the dark.

Nyxian...?

Nothing.

No voice. No words.

Just a wall of fury and something else—

Pain.

Real pain.

My knees nearly buckle.

Sadie catches me. "Breathe. Don't push too hard. The first time's always overwhelming."

My hands shake. "He's hurt."

Layla's expression hardens. "Then we find him. *Now.*"

Layla jumps to her feet, her book falling to the floor with a thunderous *clap* that echoes through the room like a war drum. She grabs Drepane without hesitation, the sickle humming in her hand like it's already hungry for a fight.

Flo lifts her massive head, yawns like a bored god, and stretches with all the lazy menace of something that knows it can end worlds if provoked. The floor shudders as she rises to her full, terrifying height.

"Get your boots," Layla says, her voice sharp as broken glass. "If something's wrong, we move."

"Where are we going?" I ask, already rushing to grab the combat boots I left by the fireplace.

Layla doesn't look at me as she straps a belt across her hips and loads it with strange little vials that shimmer with eerie, shifting color. "Wherever that feeling is coming from."

Sadie moves slower, but still rises with surprising agility for someone with a third-trimester belly. "You're not leaving me behind," she mutters, snatching a curved dagger off the mantel like it's her goddamn toothbrush.

"You're not fighting," Layla snaps.

"I can still punch someone if I have to."

Layla opens her mouth to argue, but Flo lets out a low rumble—something between a growl and a purr—and they both go silent. The tiger-beast steps closer to me, brushing her massive head against my arm like a blessing or a warning. "You're *not* coming, Sadie."

I glance at Layla. "You said to reach for him. I did. I felt pain." I am full of straight fucking panic.

Her eyes meet mine, something ancient and furious burning behind her storm-emerald stare. "We will find him."

CHAPTER THIRTY-TWO

Wynne

RUN TO YOU - PENTATONIX

The cold hits first—damp and bitter, like the land itself was burned and left to rot.

We step into a forest carved by chaos. Trees are splintered and shredded, torn from their roots like paper dolls. Blood soaks the moss beneath our feet, turning the earth black and red. Scorch marks streak the underbrush, the lingering stench of sulfur and smoke clawing at my throat.

Overhead, the sky hangs like a wound—dull red, swollen, and low, as if the whole realm is holding its breath.

Flo is the first to move. She sniffs the air and bolts forward, silent and focused, her massive form slipping through the wreckage like shadowed thunder.

"There," Layla mutters, her voice clipped and cold. "They're retreating."

Shapes emerge between the broken trees—men made of blood and bone and fury. Azrael, towering and silent, gripping Orcus with an exhausted grasp. Ashton supports a limping Vassago, whose mouth is tight with pain.

And—

Nyxian.

My body moves before I can think.

I run.

He sees me, and even through the smear of blood and ash on his face, I watch the shift—the moment something in his posture gives way. Relief. Shame. Pain. He stumbles just once before I catch him.

"Don't you *fucking dare*," I whisper as I throw my arms around him, catching the full weight of him as he leans in, bloody and broken and *mine*.

"Thought I could handle it," he mutters against my shoulder, his breath hot and strained. "Didn't want you to feel it."

"We didn't exactly have a choice," I snap, my voice cracking with fury and fear. "And I don't care what you wanted. I *felt* it, Nyx. It was like someone tore a hole through my chest."

He flinches when I pull back to look at him. Blood streaks his temple. His ribs are a ruined landscape—bruised, swollen, crusted in drying red.

"I'm okay," he lies.

"You're not," I whisper. "But you're alive. That's all I care about."

Behind us, Drepane hums louder—restless, bloodthirsty.

"Oh, *someone* will pay for this," the sickle growls, his voice metallic and sharp. "Next time, don't start the party without me."

Layla doesn't answer him. Her eyes sweep the tree line like she's cataloging ghosts.

Flo circles the group, tail twitching, hackles raised. She lets out a low growl, the kind that turns your bones to glass.

"We need to move," Layla says, Drepane already glowing brighter in her grip. "There's a ridge just beyond that rise."

"I can walk," Nyxian mutters, trying to straighten.

"Don't be a dumbass," I say, looping his arm over my shoulder again. He doesn't protest this time.

As we trudge forward, Orcus pulses against Azrael's back. The scythe's voice curls into the air like a dark wind. "Coward magic," Orcus hisses. "They didn't even *finish* the job. Pathetic."

"Shut up," Nyxian grits out.

"You know I'm right."

Drepane snorts. "You're always so dramatic. Like a theater blade with a vengeance kink."

"Don't tempt me, pretty girl."

"*Boys,*" Layla snaps. "Focus. Save your pissing contest for after we're not surrounded by cursed woods and males bleeding out."

I glance up at her, and despite the storm gathering behind her eyes, I see it—the worry. The fury. The sisterhood born not from blood, but from surviving gods and loving monsters.

Layla doesn't say anything, but her grip tightens around Drepane, and I know—she's ready to burn the fucking world down if it comes to it.

I hold Nyxian closer as we move. His weight drags heavier with every step, and I feel his pain humming through the bond like radio static—white-hot, pulsing, relentless. Every shallow breath he takes vibrates through me like a silent scream.

But beneath that pain, I feel something else.

A lifeline.

Tethered to mine.

When I close my eyes, even just for a second, I can *see* it—this invisible thread stretched taut between us, pulsing like a heartbeat. A red cord, thick and glowing, braided with something soft and luminous—pink, delicate, almost shimmering.

Our bond.

Not just a feeling now, but a visual I can grasp, something that pulses with every emotion he doesn't say out loud.

I feel him.

His love. Brutal, unyielding, burning like wildfire. His need to shield me, to protect me, to destroy anything that threatens the air in my lungs. I feel the rage that simmers when he imagines me hurt. The tenderness in the way he sees me—his Ember of Life. His *everything*.

And all I can think is... I'm not *enough*.

I'm ignorant. Untrained. Helpless to protect him the way he protects me.

My chest tightens, shame threatening to crawl up my throat, but then—

"*You're not helpless*," he rasps, voice broken and raw from pain. His head lolls against mine, but his words are sharp, defiant. "You are my fragile Ember of fucking Life, and I will *kill* anyone who poses a threat to you. I will die knowing that you are safe."

He lifts his head just enough to meet my eyes. There's blood on his lip. His gaze is fire.

"Don't mistake me, Little Disaster. I don't need protection."

His words hit me like a slap, and something in me *snaps*.

"You can't keep doing this!" I scream, the sound torn straight from my chest. "You can't just come into my life, force me to be here with you, and then *nearly die* like it's nothing! You can't fucking do this, Nyxian!"

He flinches—not from the pain in his body, but the pain in my voice.

"I didn't force you," he whispers. "You asked for this. We both did."

"You think that makes it *okay*?" My hands tighten around his waist. "You think that gives you permission to throw your life away while I stand here and *feel it* happening?"

My voice breaks.

Tears burn, but I don't let them fall.

"You didn't just almost die out there," I whisper, voice trembling. "You *hurt* me."

For a long moment, he says nothing. The trees are silent around us. Flo growls softly somewhere ahead. Layla glances back, but doesn't interrupt.

Then Nyxian leans in, forehead pressing gently against mine.

"I'm sorry," he breathes. "Not just for this. For all of it."

I hold him tighter, clinging to the lifeline that binds us.

Because this war—his war—is mine now, too.

And I swear, I will never be helpless again.

CHAPTER THIRTY-THREE

Wynne

ASHES- CELINE DION

The campfire crackles low in the center of the clearing, casting gold against the bloodied edges of the night. Layla and Flo sit close together, whispering over a small bowl of salve as Drepane leans beside them—like a quiet promise of violence. Azrael leans against a twisted tree trunk, silent and unreadable, his attention flicking between the trees and the wounds on Vassago's side as Ashton rests a steady hand over his chest, eyes closed in concentration.

They're passing energy to heal.

No fire magic. No glowing hands. Just quiet exchanges of power—like passing water from one cup to another.

It's peaceful.

And I hate it.

Because Nyxian's still in the tent.

Still not moving.

Still too quiet.

I sit just inside the open flap, knees pulled to my chest, watching him through the soft light of the lantern Layla left for me. He's pale beneath the bruises, shirt discarded so we could wrap the worst of the damage across his ribs. Bandages wind across his torso, soaked in the remnants of too much pain. His lips are parted, breathing shallow but even.

He's alive.

But I'm still shaking.

I can feel the bond—the thread braided red and pink—tugging gently between us, steady and firm like a lifeline. It anchors me, even while everything else inside me spirals.

How the fuck am I supposed to rest when I *felt* him bleed?

When I *felt* that moment of near-death like the world tried to rip him from me?

"You're staring," he rasps.

My heart slams against my ribs.

"Still half-dead and you're running your mouth?" I whisper, crawling toward him and leaning over on my elbows. "That's a good sign."

His lips twitch, the closest thing to a smile I've seen since we got here. "Didn't want to interrupt the brooding. Looked intense."

"Asshole."

"Your asshole."

My throat tightens. "Don't joke about that right now."

He blinks slowly, expression sobering. "I know."

I brush the hair from his forehead. His skin is clammy, too cold.

"I don't know how to help," I whisper. "Everyone else is passing energy. I can't heal you, Nyxian. I can't fix this."

"You're here."

He says it so simply, like that's the answer to everything. And maybe it is.

"I don't want to lose you," I say.

"You won't."

"You nearly—"

"But I didn't."

We stare at each other in the soft quiet, the bond humming steady between us like a heartbeat.

He shifts slightly, wincing. "Lie down with me."

I hesitate only a second before curling in beside him, careful of his ribs, careful of everything. He pulls me closer, despite the pain. Our foreheads touch.

"I'm not used to being the one taken care of," he mutters, voice rough, broken.

I trace my finger down his arm, slow and deliberate, watching the goose-bumps rise in my wake. "Then get used to it."

Outside, the world keeps moving—Vassago groaning, Layla laughing, someone shuffling past the fire pit. But in here, it's quiet. Dim. Heavy with the scent of blood, ash, and *him*.

And he's watching me. Through half-lidded eyes, like it's taking effort just to stay conscious, but he's still watching. For me.

"You smell like smoke," I murmur, fingers still drifting over his skin. "Like something about to catch fire."

"Maybe I am," he breathes, gaze dragging down my body, lazy and molten. "Maybe you're the match."

His words crawl down my spine like lightning.

"You should be resting," I whisper, though I don't move away.

He shifts, just barely—enough to let my hand rest over his chest.

"I *am* resting," he says, tone lower now. "You're here."

The thread between us hums, low and needy, like a guitar string plucked just beneath the surface of my skin. That red and pink braid—I *feel* it. Wrapped tight around my ribs. Around my fucking soul.

"I felt you break," I say. "I felt it, Nyxian. Don't ever do that to me again."

"I'd die for you," he says, too easily.

I press my hand harder against his chest. "I don't *want* you to die for me. I want you to *live* for me. *Stay* for me."

His hand lifts with trembling effort, cupping the back of my neck and pulling me closer. "Then kiss me, Ember. Remind me what the fuck I'm living for."

My breath catches.

He's ruined—bloodied, bandaged, shadows barely flickering—but his lips are still Nyxian's. Demanding. Hungry. *Mine.*

So I kiss him.

Not sweet. Not gentle.

Desperate.

His fingers knot in my hair like he's afraid I'll vanish. His mouth opens under mine and I swear I taste everything he can't say—pain, power, possession.

He growls into the kiss, the sound scraping up from somewhere deeper than pain. "You're playing with fire."

"You are the fire," I whisper against his lips. "I'm just learning how to burn."

His hand drops to my waist, tugging me onto him until I'm straddling his hips, careful not to touch the worst of his wounds.

I brace my hands on either side of his head, breath shallow. "Tell me to stop."

"I *will murder* anyone who tries."

"You're still bleeding."

"I've bled worse. But right now, I want to feel *you.*"

Fuck, help me—I want to give him that. Every shattered piece. Every thread of heat. Every ounce of control he's trying to pretend he still has.

I grind down just enough to make him hiss through his teeth, his eyes fluttering shut like he's torn between pleasure and pain.

"Wynne," he groans—my name like a weapon on his tongue. "I'm trying to be good."

"Don't," I whisper, dragging my mouth along his jaw, "You're not good. You've never been good."

His grip tightens on my waist, shadows flickering at his fingertips even though he's barely holding them back. "You really want to test me when I can't move without wincing?"

"I'm not testing you," I murmur, leaning in until our foreheads touch. "I'm taking care of you. My way."

I kiss him again, slower this time—softer, more control. He lets me lead, but it's killing him. I feel it in the tremble of his hands, the way his body arches beneath mine like instinct won't let him submit, even now.

He breaks the kiss first, panting. "This is torture."

"Maybe I like having you at my mercy for once," I tease, running my fingers across the edge of his bandages. "Look at you. Big bad prince of shadows, wrecked in a tent, begging for his girl."

"I'm not begging," he growls.

"Good," I smirk. "But a part of me wants to know what you look like when you do."

His shadows flicker—finally, some life in them again. They lick at the air around us like they're trying to taste me, surround me, *claim* me. And I let them. I lean into them.

"Wynne," he says again, more grounded this time. "You're playing a dangerous game."

"You made me part of this war, Nyx," I whisper against his lips. "You dragged me into your chaos. So let me love the monster too."

His breath hitches—sharp, broken. "You already do."

My hands slide under the blanket, over his abdomen—carefully, deliberately. "Then let me prove it."

His eyes burn into mine, wild and dark. "If you do this, if we do this right now, injured or not—I'm not letting you go. You understand that?"

"Nyxian," I say, lowering my mouth to his again, "I never asked you to."

His skin is still too cold.

Not in a mortal way. Not in a "get a blanket" way. It's the kind of cold that tastes like death when you breathe it in—bone-deep, magic-laced, terrifying.

And yet, when his eyes open and find mine, they're molten.

"You keep looking at me like that," Nyxian rasps, voice roughened by pain, "and I'll forget I'm supposed to be resting."

I smirk, crawling up beside him, slow and deliberate. "Then forget."

He inhales sharply as I lower myself, not onto him, not yet—but close enough that he can feel the heat radiating from me. Close enough that his breath stutters.

"You're supposed to be healing," I whisper, fingers ghosting over the bruises that crawl across his ribs like ink stains. "And yet here you are, already trying to sin your way into an early grave."

He grins through a wince, shadows twitching beneath his skin. "If everlasting sleep looks like you riding me in a tent full of ancient gods and grumpy warriors, I'll take my chances."

My palm slaps lightly over his mouth, not enough to hurt—just enough to dominate.

"Shut up," I breathe. "You don't get to talk like that when you've scared the shit out of me."

His eyes burn as I press down slightly, his breath hot beneath my fingers. I can feel him straining not to move. He could. He's stronger than me. But right now? He's letting me win. Letting me burn.

"You scared me," I say again, quieter this time. My hand slips from his mouth to his throat. My thumb brushes his Adams apple. "I felt it. Through the bond. That cold. That silence."

Nyxian doesn't blink. Doesn't breathe.

"I thought I was going to lose you," I whisper, lowering my mouth to his. "And now all I want is to ruin you."

His restraint breaks. A growl rips from his throat and his hands—fuck, his hands—dig into my thighs like he wants to fuse us together.

"You want to ruin me?" he growls. "Then do it, Little Disaster. Ruin me like I'm the fucking world that burned you."

My lips crash into his like a threat.

And I'm not careful.

Not anymore.

Because this isn't about comfort. It isn't about healing.

This is about taking back power in the only language the broken understand—need. Hunger. Pain turned into pleasure, and love laced with destruction.

His shadows return, slow and crawling, licking up my spine like smoke claiming what's his.

He may be wounded.

But I'm the fire now.

His shadows flicker—hesitant at first, like he's holding back out of instinct, out of pain. But I feel it. That tension. That restraint coiled under his skin like a beast in a cage.

"You're holding back," I murmur against his jaw, dragging my teeth just hard enough to leave a mark. "Why?"

"You know why," he growls, low and dangerous, even as his fingers dig deeper into my thighs. "You want me feral? I'll bleed for it. But you—you'll burn for it."

"Good." I rock against him, grinding slow, torturous. "Then bleed. Burn. Just don't stop."

That's what breaks him.

He surges upward—wounded or not—and flips me beneath him like instinct takes over. The breath rushes from my lungs with a startled gasp, but I don't resist. Not when his weight presses me into the ground, not when his mouth crashes into mine with the kind of hunger you don't recover from.

"Don't beg me for mercy when I make you scream," he snarls against my neck, shadows crawling from his skin to mine, marking me. Claiming me. "You asked for this, Ember. You fucking begged."

I wrap my legs around his hips and drag him down harder. "Then stop teasing me and *take* what you fucking want."

His laugh is sharp and cruel—feral. "Oh, I will."

One hand pins both of mine above my head, unforgiving. The other trails down my body with brutal precision, yanking fabric aside, baring me to the cold air and the heat of his mouth.

He doesn't worship.

He *devours*.

There's no sweetness in it—just punishment disguised as pleasure, as if every kiss, every nip, every brutal press of his body is retribution for the terror I felt when I thought I'd lost him. For making him feel weak. For making me care.

The shadows slither over my skin like smoke and silk, binding my wrists tighter, anchoring my hips in place. I can't move. I don't want to.

His mouth trails lower, and when I whimper—when I *moan*—he looks up with fire in his eyes.

"I'll remind you what I *am*," he growls, "so you never again think I can be taken from you."

"We have to go!" I hear Ashton screaming from the outside of our tent.

Nyxian growls while I groan.

"It's Sadie. She's hiding. They are trying to kill her!" The panic in Ashton's voice is overwhelming, raw.

Also by the author:

DEATH IS INEVITABLE, BUT LOVE MIGHT JUST REWRITE THE RULES...

Available on Amazon for Kindle Unlimited, Kindle, and Softback!

About the author

Peggy is a passionate author who thrives on crafting stories that delve into romance and thrillers, weaving tales that keep readers hooked until the very last page. Born on August 8, 1995, Peggy finds inspiration in life's twists and turns, as well as the works of literary icons like Penelope Douglas and Brynne Weaver. As a mother to four biological children and a loving mentor to many "adopted" kids, Peggy believes in the power of family and connection, themes that often resonate through her stories. When not writing, she enjoys exploring new creative avenues and diving into the thrill of a good book.

Pegngremlin.com

www.ingramcontent.com/pod-product-compliance
Lightning Source LLC
Chambersburg PA
CBHW071502170626
46811CB00007B/2680